PENGUIN BOOKS

MAIGRET AND THE BURGLAR'S WIFE

Georges Simenon was born at Liège in Belgium in 1903. At sixteen he began work as a journalist on the *Gazette de Liège*. He published over 212 novels in his own name, many of which belong to the Inspector Maigret series, and his work has been published in thirty-two languages. He has had a great influence upon French cinema, and more than forty of his novels have been filmed.

Simenon's novels are largely psychological. He describes hidden fears, tensions and alliances beneath the surface of life's ordinary routine which suddenly explode into violence and crime. André Gide called him 'perhaps the greatest and most genuine *romancier* of today's French literature', and François Mauriac wrote, 'I am afraid I may not have the courage to descend right to the depths of this nightmare which Simenon describes with such unendurable art'.

Simenon travelled a great deal and once lived on a cutter, making long journeys of exploration round the coasts of Northern Europe. A book of reminiscences, *Letter to My Mother*, was published in England in 1976.

Georges Simenon died in 1989. In his obituary *The Times* wrote that 'His main achievement was . . . to turn the simplest of *romans policiers* into a moving and memorable form of art', while the *Sunday Times* described him as 'unique, disrupting hitherto hallowed ground . . . He summoned up characters . . . and their various physical environments like a wizard of life, lending the everyday a miraculous and exotic immediacy.'

MAIGRET AND
THE BURGLAR'S WIFE

GEORGES SIMENON

TRANSLATED
FROM THE FRENCH BY
J. MACLAREN-ROSS

PENGUIN BOOKS

PENGUIN BOOKS

Published by the Penguin Group
Penguin Books Ltd, 27 Wrights Lane, London w8 5tz, England
Penguin Books USA Inc., 375 Hudson Street, New York New York 10014, USA
Penguin Books Australia Ltd, Ringwood, Victoria, Australia
Penguin Books Canada Ltd, 10 Alcorn Avenue, Toronto, Ontario, Canada m4v 3b2
Penguin Books (NZ) Ltd, 182–190 Wairau Road, Auckland 10, New Zealand

Penguin Books Ltd, Registered Offices: Harmondsworth, Middlesex, England

Maigret et la grand perche first published 1953
First published in Great Britain as *Maigret and the Burglar's Wife* by Hamish Hamilton 1955
Published in Penguin Books 1959
5 7 9 10 8 6

Copyright 1953 by Georges Simenon
Translation copyright © Hamish Hamilton Ltd, 1955
All rights reserved

Printed in England by Clays Ltd, St Ives plc
Filmset in Garamond

Chapter One

THE appointment-slip, duly filled in, and handed to Maigret by the office porter, bore the following text:

Ernestine Micou, alias 'Lofty' (now Jussiaume), who, when you arrested her seventeen years ago in the Rue de la Lune, stripped herself naked to take the mike out of you, requests the favour of an interview on a matter of most urgent and important business.

Maigret glanced quickly, out of the corner of his eye, at old Joseph, to see whether he'd read the message, but the white-haired 'boy' didn't move a muscle. He was probably the only one in the whole of Police Headquarters that morning who wasn't in shirt-sleeves, and for the first time in so many years the Chief-Inspector wondered by what official vagary this almost venerable man was compelled to wear a heavy chain with a huge seal round his neck.

It was the sort of day when one's apt to indulge in pointless speculation. The heat-wave may have been to blame. Perhaps the holiday spirit also prevented one from taking things very seriously. The windows were wide open and the muted roar of Paris throbbed in the room where, before Joseph came in, Maigret had been engaged in following the flight of a wasp that was going round in circles and bumping against the ceiling at invariably the same spot. At least half the plain-clothes section was at the seaside or in the country. Lucas went about wearing a straw hat which, on him, assumed the aspect of a native grass hat or a lampshade. The Chief himself had left the day before, as he did year after year, for the Pyrenees.

'Drunk?' Maigret asked the porter.

'Don't think so, sir.'

For a certain type of woman, having taken a drop too much, often feels impelled to make disclosures to the police.

'Jumpy?'

'She asked me if it'd take long, and I said I didn't even know if you'd see her. She sat herself down in a corner of the waiting-room and started to read the paper.'

Maigret couldn't recall the names Micou or Jussiaume, or even the nickname Lofty, but he retained a vivid memory of the Rue de la Lune, on a day as hot as this, when the asphalt feels elastic under one's tread and fills Paris with a smell of tar.

It was down by the Porte Saint-Denis, a little street of shady hotels and small sweet-shops. He wasn't a Chief-Inspector in those days. The women wore low-waisted frocks and had shingled hair. To find out about this girl, he'd had to go into two or three of the neighbouring bars, and it so happened he'd been drinking Pernod. He could almost conjure up the smell of it, just as he could conjure up the smell of armpits and feet pervading the small hotel. The room was on the third or fourth floor. Mistaking the door, he'd first of all found himself face to face with a negro who, sitting on his bed, was playing the accordion; one of the band in a *bal musette*, probably. Quite unperturbed, the negro had indicated the room next door with a jerk of his chin.

'Come in!'

A husky voice. The voice of one who drank or smoked too much. And, standing by a window that gave on to the courtyard, a tall girl in a sky-blue wrap, cooking herself a chop on a spirit lamp.

She was as tall as Maigret, maybe taller. She'd looked him up and down without emotion; she'd said straight away:

'You're a copper?'

He'd found the pocket-book and the bank-notes on top of the wardrobe, and she hadn't batted an eyelid.

'It was my girl friend who did the job.'

'What girl friend?'

'Don't know her name. Lulu, they call her.'

6

'Where is she?'

'Find out. That's your business.'

'Get dressed and come with me.'

It was only a case of petty theft, but Headquarters took a rather serious view of it, not so much because of the sum involved, though this was a pretty large one, as because it concerned a big cattle-dealer from the Charentes, who had already started to stir up his local Deputy.

'It'd take more than you to stop me eating my chop!'

The tiny room contained only one chair. He'd remained standing while the girl ate, taking her time; he might not have been there for all the attention she paid to him.

She must have been rising twenty at the time. She was pale, with colourless eyes, a long bony face. He could see her now, picking her teeth with a matchstick, then pouring boiling water into the coffee-pot.

'I asked you to get dressed.'

He was hot. The smell of the hotel turned his stomach. Had she sensed that he was not at his ease?

Calmly she'd taken off her wrap, her shift, and pants, and, stark naked, had gone and lain down on the unmade bed, lighting a cigarette.

'I'm waiting!' he'd told her impatiently, looking away with an effort.

'So am I.'

'I've a warrant for your arrest.'

'Well, arrest me then!'

'Get dressed and come along.'

'I'm all right like this.'

The whole thing was ludicrous. She was cool, quite passive, a little glint of irony showing in her colourless eyes.

'You say I'm under arrest. *I* don't mind. But you needn't ask me to give you a hand as well. I'm in my own place. It's hot, and I've a right to take my clothes off. Now, if you insist on my coming along with you just as I am, I'm not complaining.'

At least a dozen times he'd told her:

'Get your things on!'

And, perhaps because of her pallid flesh, perhaps because of the surrounding squalor, it seemed to him that he'd never seen a woman so naked as that. To no avail he'd thrown her clothes on the bed, had threatened her, then tried persuasiveness.

In the end he'd gone down and fetched two policemen, and the scene had become farcical. They'd had to wrap the girl forcibly in a blanket and carry her, like a packing-case, down the narrow staircase, while all the doors opened as they went by.

He'd never seen her since. He'd never heard her mentioned.

'Send her in!' he sighed.

He knew her at once. She didn't seem to have changed. He recognized her long pale face, the washed-out eyes, the big over-made-up mouth that looked like a raw wound. He recognized also, in her glance, the quiet irony of those who've seen so much that nothing's any longer important in their eyes.

She was simply dressed, with a light green straw hat, and she'd put on gloves.

'Still got it in for me?'

He drew on his pipe without answering.

'Can I have a seat? I heard you'd been promoted and in fact that's why I never ran into you again. Is it all right if I smoke?'

She took a cigarette from her bag and lit up.

'I want to tell you right away, and with no hard feelings, that I was telling the truth that time. I got a year inside that I didn't deserve. There was a girl called Lulu all right, whom you didn't take the trouble to find. The two of us were together when we ran across that fat steamer. He picked us both up, but when he'd taken a good look at me, he told me to buzz off because he couldn't stand 'em skinny. I was outside in the passage when Lulu slipped me the pocket-book an hour after so's I could ditch it.'

'What became of her?'

'Five years ago she'd a little restaurant down South. I just wanted to show you everyone sometimes makes mistakes.'

'Is that why you came?'

'No. I wanted to talk to you about Alfred. If he knew I was here, he'd take me for a proper mug. I could've gone to Sergeant Boissier, who knows all about him.'

'Who's Alfred?'

'My husband. Lawfully wedded, too, before the mayor *and* the vicar, because he still goes to church. Sergeant Boissier pinched him two or three times, and one of those times he got Alfred five years in Fresnes.'

Her voice was almost harsh.

'The name Jussiaume doesn't mean much to you, perhaps, but when I tell you what they call him, you'll know who he is right away. There's been a lot about him in the papers. He's Sad Freddie.'

'Safe-breaking?'

'Yes.'

'You've had a row?'

'No. It's not what you'd think I've come for. I'm not that sort. So you see who Fred is now?'

Maigret had never set eyes on him, or, rather, only in the corridors, when the cracksman was waiting to be interrogated by Boissier. He called to mind vaguely a puny little man with anxious eyes, whose clothes seemed too big for his scrawny body.

'Of course, we don't look at him the same way,' she said. 'Poor blighter. There's more to him than you think. I've lived with him close on twelve years; I'm only starting to get to know him.'

'Where is he?'

'I'm coming to that, don't worry. I don't know where he is, but he's got in a proper jam without its being any of his fault, and that's why I'm here. Only you've simply got to trust me, and I know that's asking a lot.'

He was watching her with interest, because she spoke with appealing simplicity. She wasn't putting on airs, wasn't trying to impress him. If she took some time in coming to the point, it was because what she had to tell was genuinely complicated.

There was still a barrier between them, nevertheless, and it was this barrier that she was trying hard to break down, so that he wouldn't get a wrong idea of things.

About Sad Freddie, with whom he'd never had any personal dealings, Maigret knew little more than he'd heard at Headquarters. The man was a sort of celebrity, and the newspapers had tried their best to boost him into a romantic figure.

He'd been employed for years by the firm of Planchart, the safe-makers, and had become one of their most skilled workers. He was, even at that time, a sad, retiring youth, in poor health, throwing epileptic fits periodically.

Boissier would probably be able to tell Maigret how he had come to give up his job at Planchart's.

Whatever the cause, he had turned from installing safes to cracking them.

'When you first met him, had he still got a steady job?'

'Not likely. It wasn't me that sent him off the straight and narrow, in case that's what you've got in mind. He was doing odd jobs, sometimes he'd hire himself out to a locksmith, but it wasn't long before I saw what he was really up to.'

'You don't think you'd do better to see Boissier?'

'Housebreaking's his line, isn't it? But you deal with murder.'

'Has Alfred killed anybody?'

'Look, Chief-Inspector, I think we'll get along faster if you just let me talk. Alfred may be anything you'd like to call him, but he wouldn't murder for all the money in the world. May seem soppy to say so about a bloke like him, but he's sensitive, see? Why, he'd pipe his eyes for the least little thing. I ought to know. Anyone else would say he was soft. But maybe it's because he's like that, that I fell in love with him.'

And she looked at him quietly. She'd uttered the word 'love' without particular emphasis, but with a sort of pride all the same.

'If one knew what was going on in his head, one wouldn't half get a surprise. Not that it matters. Far's you're concerned, he's just a thief. He got himself pinched once and did five years inside. I never missed going to see him a single visiting-day, and all that time I'd to go back on my old beat, at the risk of getting in trouble, not having a proper card and those being the days when you still had to have one.

'He always hopes he'll pull off a big job and then we can go and live in the country. He's always dreamed of it ever since he was a nipper.'

'Where do you live?'

'On the Quai de Jemmapes, just opposite the Saint-Martin Lock. Know where I mean? We've two rooms above a café painted green, and it's very handy because of the phone.'

'Is Alfred there now?'

'No. I already told you I don't know where he is, and believe me I don't. He did a job, not last night, but the night before.'

'And he's cleared out?'

'Hang on, will you, Inspector? You'll see later on that everything I tell you's got its point. You know people that take tickets in the National Sweep at every draw, don't you? There are some of them that go without eating to buy them, because they reckon in a day or two they'll be in the money at last. Well, that's the way it is with Alfred. There're dozens of safes in Paris that he put in himself, and that he knows like the back of his hand. Usually, when you buy a safe, it's to put money or jewels away in.'

'He hopes to strike lucky one day?'

'You got it.'

She shrugged, as though speaking of a child's harmless craze. Then she added:

'He's just unlucky. Most times it's title-deeds it's impossible to sell or else business contracts he gets hold of. Only once there was real big dough, that he could've lived on quietly for the rest of his days, and that time Boissier pinched him.'

'Were you with him? Do you keep the look-out?'

'No. He never liked me to. At the start, he used to tell me where he was going to be on the job, and I'd fix it so I was near by. When he spotted that, he gave up telling me anything.'

'For fear you'd get pulled in?'

'Maybe. Or it may have been because he's superstitious. See, even when we're living together, he's all alone really, and sometimes he doesn't say a word for two whole days. When I see him go out at night on his bicycle, I know what's up.'

Maigret remembered this characteristic. Some of the newspapers had dubbed Alfred Jussiaume the burglar-on-a-bike.

'That's another of his notions. He reckons that nobody, at night, is going to notice a man on a bike, specially if he's got a bag of tools slung over his shoulder. They'd take him for a bloke on his way to work. I'm talking to you like I would to a friend, see?'

Maigret wondered again why she had really come to his office and, as she took out another cigarette, he held a lighted match for her.

'We're Thursday today. On Tuesday night Alfred went out on a job.'

'Did he tell you so?'

'He'd been going out for several nights at the same time, and that's always a sign. Before breaking into a house or an office, he sometimes spends a week on the watch to get to know the people's habits.'

'And to make sure there'll be no one about?'

'No. That doesn't signify to him. I even think he'd rather work where there was somebody than in an empty house. He's a bloke that can get about without making a sound. Why, hundreds of times he's slipped into bed beside me at night and I never so much as knew he'd come home.'

'D'you know where he worked the night before last?'

'All I know, it was at Neuilly. And then I only found it out by chance. The day before, when I came in, he told me the police had asked to see his papers, and must've taken him for a dirty old man because they stopped him in the Bois de Boulogne, just by the place where women go and tidy up.

'"Where was it?" I asked him.

'"Behind the Zoo. I was coming back from Neuilly."

'Then, night before last, he took his bag of tools, and I knew he'd gone to work.'

'He hadn't been drinking?'

'Never touches a drop, doesn't smoke. He'd never be able to take it. He lives in terror of his fits, and he's that ashamed when it happens in the middle of the street, with masses of people who crowd round and feel sorry for him. He said to me before he set out:

'"I reckon this time we're really going down to live in the country."'

Maigret had begun to take notes which he was surrounding automatically with arabesques.

'What time did he leave the Quai de Jemmapes?'

'About eleven, like on the other nights.'

'Then he must have got to Neuilly round about midnight.'

'Maybe. He never rode fast, but then, at that time, there'd be no traffic.'

'When did you see him again?'

'I haven't seen him again.'

'So you think something may have happened to him?'

'He rang me up.'

'When?'

'Five in the morning. I wasn't asleep. I was worried. If he's always scared he'll have a fit in the street, I'm always scared it might happen while he's working, you see? I heard the phone ringing downstairs in the café. Our room's right up above. The owners didn't get up. I guessed it was for me, and I went down. I knew right away from his voice there'd been a hitch. He spoke very low.

'"That you?"

'"Yes!"

'"Are you alone?"

'"Yes. Where are you?"

'"In a little café up by the Gare du Nord. Look, Tine," (he always calls me Tine), "I've simply got to make myself scarce for a bit."

'"Somebody see you?"

'"It's not that. I don't know. A bloke saw me, yes, but I'm not sure it was a policeman."

'"Got any money?"

'"No. It happened before I'd finished."

'"What happened?"

'"I was busy on the lock when my torch lit up a face in the corner of the room. I thought somebody'd come in silently and was watching me. Then I saw the eyes were dead."'

She watched Maigret.

'I'm sure he wasn't lying. If he'd killed anyone, he'd have told me. And I'm not going telling you any stories. I could tell he was near fainting at the other end. He's so scared of death ...'

'Who was it?'

'I don't know. He didn't make it very clear. He was going to hang up the whole time. He was scared someone'd hear him. He told me he was taking a train in a quarter of an hour ...'

'To Belgium?'

'Probably, as he was near the Gare du Nord. I looked up a time-table. There's a train at five forty-five.'

'You've no more idea what café he was phoning from?'

'I went on a scout round the district yesterday and asked some questions, but no good. They must've taken me for a jealous wife, and they weren't giving anything away.'

'So all he really told you was that there was a dead body in the room where he was working?'

'I got him to tell me a bit more. He said it was a woman, that her chest was all covered in blood, and that she was holding a telephone receiver in her hand.'

'Is that all?'

'No. Just as he was going to do a bunk – and I can imagine the state he was in! – a car drew up in front of the gate ...'

'You're sure he said the gate?'

'Yes. A wrought-iron gate. I remember it struck me particularly. Somebody got out and came towards the door. As the man went into the passage, Alfred got out of the house by the window.'

'And his tools?'

'He'd left them behind. He'd cut out a window-pane to get in. That I'm sure of, because he always does. I believe he'd do it even if the door was open, he's sort of faddy that way, or maybe superstitious.'

'So nobody saw him?'

'Yes. As he was going through the garden ...'

'He mentioned a garden as well?'

'I didn't make it up. As I say, just when he was going through the garden someone looked out of the window and shone a torch on him; maybe Alfred's own, which he hadn't taken with him. He jumped on his bike, went off without looking round, rode down as far as the Seine, I don't know exactly where, and threw the bike in, for fear they'd recognize him by it. He didn't dare come back home. He got to the Gare du Nord on foot and phoned me, begging me not to say a word. I pleaded with him not to clear off. I tried to reason with him. He finished up promising to write me poste restante saying where he'd be so I could go and join him.'

'He hasn't written yet?'

'There hasn't been time for a letter to get here. I went to the post office this morning. I've had twenty-four hours to think things over. I bought all the papers, thinking they'd surely say something about a murdered woman.'

Maigret picked up the telephone and called the police-station at Neuilly.

'Hello! Headquarters here. Any murder to report during the last twenty-four hours?'

'One moment, sir. I'll put you through to the desk. I'm only the duty constable.'

Maigret persisted for some time.

'No corpse found on the roads? No night calls? No bodies fished up from the Seine?'

'Absolutely nothing, Monsieur Maigret.'

'Nobody reported a shot?'

'Nobody.'

Lofty waited patiently, like someone making a social call, both hands clasped upon her bag.

'You realize why I came to you?'

'I think so.'

'First, I reckoned the police had maybe seen Alfred, and, in that case, his bike alone would have given him away. Then there were the tools he left behind. Now he's bolted over the frontier, no one'll ever believe his story. And he's no safer in Belgium or Holland than in Paris. I'd sooner see him in jail for attempted burglary, even if it meant five years all over again, than see him had up for murder.'

'The trouble,' Maigret retorted, 'is that there's no body.'

'You think he made it up or that I'm making it up?'

He didn't answer.

'It'll be easy for you to find the house he was working in that night. Maybe I shouldn't tell you this, but I'm sure you'll think of it yourself. The safe's bound to be one of those he put in at some time. Planchart's must keep a list of their customers. There can't be that many in Neuilly who bought a safe at least seventeen years back.'

'Apart from you, did Alfred have any girl-friends?'

'Ah! I guessed that was coming. I'm not jealous and, even if I was, I wouldn't come to you with a pack of lies to get my own back, if that's what you've got in mind. He hasn't a girl-friend because he doesn't want one, poor blighter. If he wanted to I'm the one who'd fix him up with as much as he liked.'

'Why?'

'Because life's not so much cop for him, as it is.'

'Have you any money?'

'No.'

'What are you going to do?'

'I'll get by, you know that all right. I only came here because I want it proved that Freddie didn't kill anyone.'

'If he wrote to you, would you show me his letter?'

'You'll read it before I do. Now that you know he's going to write me poste restante, you'll have every post office in Paris watched. You forget that I know the racket.'

She had risen to her feet, very tall; she looked him over as he sat at his desk, from top to toe.

'If all the tales they tell about you are true, there's an even chance that you'll believe me.'

'Why?'

'Because otherwise you'd be a mug. And you're not one. Are you going to ring Planchart's?'

'Yes.'

'You'll keep me posted?'

He looked at her without replying, and realized that he couldn't restrain himself from smiling good-humouredly.

'Please yourself then,' she sighed. 'I could help you; you may know an awful lot, but there're things people like us understand better than you do.'

Her 'us' obviously stood for a whole world, the one that Lofty lived in, the world on the other side of the barrier.

'If Sergeant Boissier's not on holiday, I'm sure he'll bear me out in what I told you about Alfred.'

'He's not on leave. He's going tomorrow.'

She opened her bag, took from it a bit of paper.

'I'll leave you the phone number of the café underneath where we live. If by some fluke you need to come and see me, don't be scared that I'll start undressing. Nowadays, if it's left to me, I keep my clothes on!'

There was a touch of bitterness in her tone, but not much. A second later she was poking fun at herself:

'Much better for all concerned!'

It wasn't until he closed the door behind her that Maigret realized he had shaken, quite as a matter of course, the hand she'd held out to him. The wasp still buzzed in circles at ceiling level, as though seeking a way out, without thinking of the wide open windows. Madame Maigret had announced in the morning that she'd be coming round to the flower market and had asked him, if he were free about noon, to go and meet her there. It was noon now. He paused irresolute, leant out of the window from which he could see the splashes of vivid colour beyond the embankment of the quay.

Then he picked up the telephone with a sigh.

'Ask Boissier to drop in and see me.'

Seventeen years had slipped by since the absurd incident in the Rue de la Lune, and Maigret was now an important official in charge of the Homicide Branch. A funny notion came into his head, an almost childish craving. He picked up the telephone once more.

'The Brasserie Dauphine, please.'

As the door opened to admit Boissier, he was saying:

'Send me up a Pernod, will you?'

And, looking at the Sergeant, who had large half-moons of sweat on his shirt underneath the arms, he changed it to:

'Make it two! Two Pernods, thank you.'

The blue-black moustache of Boissier, who came from Provence, twitched with pleasure, and he went over to sit on the window-sill, mopping his forehead.

Chapter Two

AFTER swallowing a mouthful of Pernod, Maigret had to come to the point:

'Tell me, Boissier, old man, what d'you know about Alfred Jussiaume?'

'Sad Freddie?'

'Yes.'

And immediately the Sergeant's brow had darkened, he'd shot Maigret a worried glance, had asked in a voice no longer the same, forgetting to take a sip of his favourite drink:

'Has he done a job?'

It was always like this with the Sergeant, Maigret knew. He also knew why and, by using the utmost tact, had become the only Chief-Inspector to find favour in Boissier's eyes.

The latter, by rights, ought to have been one himself, and would have been a long time ago, had an absolute inability to spell and the handwriting of a first-form schoolboy not prevented his passing the simplest examinations.

For once, however, the administrative staff had not made a bloomer. They had appointed at the head of his branch Chief-Inspector Peuchet, an old has-been, always half-asleep and, save for drawing up the reports, it was Boissier who got through all the work and governed his colleagues.

That department wasn't concerned with homicide, as Maigret's was. It wasn't concerned with amateurs either, shop-assistants who run off one fine day with the till, or any tripe of that sort.

The customers Boissier and his men dealt with were professional thieves of every kind, from the jewel robbers who put up at the big hotels in the Champs-Élysées, to the banksmashers and hustlers, who hid out mostly, like Jussiaume, in seedy neighbourhoods.

Because of this, they had an outlook quite different from that of the Special Division. In Boissier's line, they were all craftsmen, on both sides. The battle was a battle between experts. It wasn't so much a question of psychology, as of knowing, from A to Z, the little quirks and eccentricities of everyone.

It was not unusual to see the Sergeant sitting quietly outside a café with a cat-burglar, and Maigret, for one, would have found it hard to hold a conversation of this sort with a murderer:

'Here, Julot, it's a long time since you did a job of work.'

'That's right, Sergeant.'

'When was the last time I pulled you in?'

'Must be going on six months, now.'

'Funds getting low, eh? I'll bet you're cooking something up.'

The idea that Sad Freddie might have done a bust without his knowledge put Boissier's back up.

'I don't know if he's really been on the job lately, but Lofty has just left my office.'

That was enough to reassure the Sergeant.

'She doesn't know a thing,' he stated. 'Alfred's not the type to go blabbing his business to a woman, not even his own wife.'

The picture of Jussiaume that Boissier now set himself to draw was not unlike that previously outlined by Ernestine, even though he, the Sergeant, tended rather to emphasize the professional angle.

'I get browned off with pinching a bloke like that and sending him to the nick. Last time, when they dished him out five years, I damn nearly gave his lawyer a piece of my mind for not knowing how to go about his job. He's wanting, that lawyer is!'

It was hard to define precisely what Boissier meant by 'wanting', but the point was plain enough.

'There's not another in Paris like Alfred for breaking into a house full of people without a sound and going to work there without even waking the cat. Technically, he's an artist. What's more, he doesn't need anyone to tip him off, keep a look-out and all that palaver. He works on his own, without ever getting jumpy. He doesn't drink, doesn't talk, doesn't go acting tough round the bars. With his talents he ought to have enough dough to choke himself with. He knows just where to find hundreds of safes that he put in himself, and exactly how they work, and you'd think he'd only have to go and help himself. Instead, every time he has a go, he comes a cropper or else gets a spell inside.'

Perhaps Boissier only spoke thus because he saw a parallel between Sad Freddie's career and his own, except that he himself enjoyed a constitution that could withstand any number of *apéritifs* imbibed on café terraces and nights spent standing to in all kinds of weather.

'The joke is that, if they put him away for ten years or twenty years, he'd start all over again directly he came out, even supposing he was seventy and on crutches by then. He's got it into his head that he only needs one lucky break, just one, and that he's earned it by this time.'

'He's had a nasty knock,' Maigret explained. 'It seems that he was just getting a safe open, somewhere at Neuilly, when he spotted a dead body in the room.'

'What'd I tell you? That could only happen to him. Then he cleared off? What'd he do with the bike?'

'In the Seine.'

'He's in Belgium?'

'I dare say.'

'I'll ring through to Brussels, unless you don't want him picked up?'

'I want him picked up most decidedly.'

'D'you know where this took place?'

'I know that it was at Neuilly, and that the house has a garden with a wrought-iron gate in front.'

'That'll be easy. Be back right away.'

Maigret had the grace to order, in his absence, two more Pernods from the Brasserie Dauphine. It brought back to him not only a whiff of the Rue de la Lune period, but a whiff of the South of France, particularly of a little dive in Cannes, where he'd once been on a case and, all of a sudden, the whole business was lifted out of the general rut, took on almost the aspect of a holiday task.

He hadn't definitely promised Madame Maigret to meet her in the flower market, and she knew that she ought never to wait for him. Boissier returned with a file, from which he produced, first of all, the official photographs of Alfred Jussiaume.

'That's what he looks like!'

An ascetic face, really, rather than that of a guttersnipe. The skin was stretched tight across the bones, the nostrils were long and pinched, and the stare had an almost mystical intensity. Even in these harshly lit photographs, full face and side view, collarless, with a protruding Adam's apple, the man's immense loneliness made itself felt, and his sadness that was still in no way aggressive.

Born to be fair game, it had been natural for him to be hunted.

'Would you like me to read you his record?'

'It's not necessary today. I'd rather go over the file with an open mind. What I'd like to have is the list.'

Boissier was pleased by this last sentence. Maigret knew that he would be, as he said it, for he intended it as a tribute to the Sergeant.

'You knew I'd have it?'

'I was certain you would.'

For, in point of fact, Boissier really did know his job. The list in question was that, drawn from the books of Messrs Planchart, of the safes installed in Alfred Jussiaume's time.

'Wait till I look up Neuilly. You're sure it's at Neuilly?'

'I've Ernestine's word for it.'

22

'You know, she wasn't really so dumb to come and look you up. But why you?'

'Because I arrested her, sixteen or seventeen years ago, and because she played me quite a dirty trick.'

This didn't surprise Boissier, it was all in the game. They both knew where they stood. From the glasses, the pale-coloured Pernod could already be smelt all over the office, inciting the wasp to a kind of frenzy.

'A bank ... it's certainly not that ... Freddie never took to banks, because he's windy of the burglar-alarms ... A petrol company that's been out of business for ten years ... A scent manufacturer ... he went bankrupt a year ago.'

Boissier's finger came to a stop finally on a name, on an address.

'Guillaume Serre, dentist, 43b Rue de la Ferme, Neuilly. You know it? It's just past the Zoo, a street parallel with Boulevard Richard-Wallace.'

'I know.'

They looked at each other for a moment.

'Busy?' asked Maigret.

And in so doing he was again pandering deliberately to Boissier's self-esteem.

'I was classifying some files. I'm off to Brittany tomorrow.'

'Shall we go?'

'I'll get my coat and hat. Shall I phone Brussels first?'

'Yes. And Holland as well.'

'Right you are.'

They went there by bus, standing on the outside platform. Then, in the Rue de la Ferme, quiet and countrified, they found a little café-restaurant where there were four tables on the terrace between green potted plants, and sat down there for lunch.

There were only three bricklayers in white smocks inside, drinking red wine with their meal. Flies circled round Maigret and Boissier. Farther along, on the other side of the road, they could see a black wrought-iron gate that should correspond with No. 43b.

They weren't in any hurry. If there'd really been a dead body in the house, the murderer had had over twenty-four hours in which to get rid of it.

A waitress in a black dress and a white apron looked after them, but the proprietor came over to greet them.

'Nice weather, gentlemen.'

'Nice weather. Would you, by any chance, know of a dentist anywhere about here?'

A sidelong nod.

'There's one opposite, over there, but I don't know what he's like. My missus prefers to go to one in the Boulevard Sebastopol. This one'd be expensive, I'd say. He hasn't all that many patients.'

'D'you know him?'

'A wee bit.'

The proprietor paused, looking them over for a while, particularly Boissier.

'You'd be police-officers, eh?'

Maigret thought it better to say yes.

'Has he done anything?'

'We're just making a few inquiries. What does he look like?'

'Taller and bigger than you and me,' he said, looking this time at the Chief-Inspector. 'I weight fifteen stone ten, and he must go all of sixteen.'

'How old?'

'Fifty? Round about, anyway. Not too well turned out, which is odd, him being a dentist. Seedy looking, like what old bachelors get.'

'He isn't married?'

'Wait a bit ... Matter of fact, if I remember rightly, he did get married, it'd be about two years ago ... There's an old woman living in the house, too – his mother, I suppose – who does the shopping every morning ...'

'No maid?'

24

'Only a charwoman. Mind you, I wouldn't be sure. I only know him because he comes in here now and then for a foxy drink.'

'Foxy?'

'In a manner of speaking. People like him don't come to places like this, as a rule. And when he does, he always takes a quick look round at his house, as if to make sure he can't be seen. And he looks sheepish, coming up to the counter.

'"Glass of red wine!" he'll say.

'Never takes anything else. I know right away not to put the bottle back on the shelf, because he's bound to have another. He drinks 'em at a gulp, wipes his mouth, and he's got the change all ready in his hand.'

'Does he ever get drunk?'

'Never. Just the two glasses. As he goes out, I see him slip a cachou or a clove into his mouth, so that his breath won't smell of wine.'

'What's his mother like?'

'A little old woman, very dried up, dressed in black, who never passes the time of day with anybody and doesn't look easy to get on with.'

'His wife?'

'I've scarcely seen her except when they go by in the car, but I've heard tell she's a foreigner. She's tall and stout like him, with a high colour.'

'D'you think they're away on holiday?'

'Let's see. I believe I still served him with his two glasses of red two or three days ago.'

'Two or three?'

'Wait a bit. It was the evening when the plumber came to mend the beer-pump. I'll go and ask my wife, to make sure I'm not talking through my hat.'

It was two days previously, in other words Tuesday, a few hours before Alfred Jussiaume discovered a dead woman's body in the house.

'Can you remember the time?'

'He comes, as a rule, about half-past six.'

'On foot?'

'Yes. They've got an old car, but that's the time of day he takes his constitutional. You can't tell me what this is all about?'

'It's not about anything at all. A check-up.'

The man didn't believe them, you could see it plainly in his eyes.

'You'll be back?'

And, turning to the Chief-Inspector: 'You're not Monsieur Maigret, by any chance?'

'Did someone say so?'

'One of the bricklayers thought he recognized you. If you are, my wife'd be very happy to meet you in the flesh.'

'We'll be back,' he promised.

They'd had a jolly good meal, and they'd drunk the Calvados which the proprietor, who came from Falaise, had offered them. Now they were talking together down the pavement on the shady side of the street. Maigret was taking little puffs at his pipe. Boissier had lit a cigarette, and two fingers of his right hand were stained brown with nicotine, coloured like a meerschaum pipe.

One might have been fifty miles outside Paris, in almost any small town. There were more private houses than buildings with flats, and some were big middle-class family mansions about a century or two old.

There was only the one gate in the street, a black wrought-iron gate beyond which a lawn was spread like a green carpet in the sunshine. On the brass plate was the legend:

GUILLAUME SERRE
Dental Surgeon

And, in smaller letters:

From 2 to 5 p.m.
By appointment only

The sun struck full on the façade of the house, warming its yellowish stone, and, except for two of the windows, the

26

shutters were closed. Boissier could sense that Maigret was undecided.

'Are you going in?'

'What have we got to lose?'

Before crossing over, he cast a quick glance up and down the street and suddenly frowned. Boissier looked in the direction towards which Maigret was gazing so steadily.

'Lofty!' he exclaimed.

She'd just come from the Boulevard Richard-Wallace, and was wearing the same green hat as earlier that morning. Catching sight of Maigret and the Sergeant, she paused for a moment, then made straight for them.

'Surprised to see me?'

'You've got hold of the address?'

'I phoned your office about half an hour ago. I wanted to tell you that I'd found the list. I knew it must be somewhere about. I've seen Alfred looking at it, and putting in crosses here and there. When I came out of your office this morning, I thought of a place where Alfred might have hidden it.'

'Where?'

'Do I have to tell you?'

'It might be as well.'

'I'd rather not. Not right away.'

'What else did you find?'

'How d'you know I found anything else?'

'You'd no money this morning and you came here by cab.'

'You're right. There was some money.'

'A lot?'

'More than I'd have expected.'

'Where's the list?'

'I burnt it.'

'Why?'

'Because of the crosses. They might have marked the places where Alfred worked and, whatever else, I'm not going to give you evidence against him.'

27

She glanced at the house.

'You going in?'

Maigret nodded.

'D'you mind if I wait for you outside the café?'

She hadn't said a word to Boissier, who, for his part, was staring at her rather sternly.

'Please yourself,' Maigret told her.

And, followed by the Sergeant, he crossed from the shade into the sunlight, while the tall figure of Ernestine moved off towards the café terrace.

It was ten past two. Unless the dentist had gone on holiday, he ought, according to the brass plate, to be waiting for patients in his surgery. There was an electric bell-push on the right of the gateway. Maigret pressed it and the gate swung open automatically. They crossed the small garden and found another bell-push by the front door, which was not mechanically operated. After the peal of the bell inside, there was a long silence. The two men listened, both of them aware that someone was lurking on the other side of the panel, and looked at each other. At last a chain was unhooked, the bolt withdrawn, a thin crack showed round the lintel of the door.

'Have you an appointment?'

'We'd like to speak to Monsieur Serre.'

'He only sees people by appointment.'

The crack did not widen. They could dimly make out, behind it, a silhouette, the thin face of an old woman.

'According to the brass plate ...'

'The plate is twenty-five years old.'

'Would you tell your son that Chief-Inspector Maigret wishes to see him?'

The door remained for a moment longer without moving, then opened; it revealed a wide hallway with a black-and-white tessellated floor which resembled that of a convent corridor, and the old lady who stood back to let them enter would not have looked out of place dressed as a nun.

'You must excuse me, Chief-Inspector, but my son doesn't really care to receive casual patients.'

The woman was far from unpresentable. She'd an innate elegance and dignity which were remarkable. She was attempting to efface by her smile any bad impression that she might have created.

'Do please come in. I'm afraid that I'll have to ask you to wait a moment or two. For some years, my son has been accustomed, especially in summer, to take a siesta, and he's still lying down. If you'd care to come this way ...'

She opened, on the left, a pair of polished oaken doors, and Maigret was reminded more than ever of a convent or, better still, a rich parsonage. Even the soft, insidious smell reminded him of something; he didn't know what, he tried to remember. The drawing-room that she showed them into was lit only by daylight seeping through the slots of the shutters, and to enter it from outside was like stepping into a cool bath.

The noises of the town, one felt, could never penetrate this far, and it was as if the house and everything in it had remained unchanged for more than a century, that the tapestried chairs, the occasional tables, the piano, and the chinaware had always stood in the same place. Even the enlarged photographs on the walls, in black wooden frames, which looked like photographs from the time of Nadar. The man strapped into a collar of the last century, above the chimney-piece, wore bushy side-whiskers and, on the opposite wall, a woman of about forty, her hair parted in the middle, looked like the Empress Eugénie.

The old lady, who might almost have stepped herself out of one of those frames, hovered at their side, motioned them to seats, folded her hands like a Sister of Mercy.

'I don't wish to seem inquisitive, Chief-Inspector. My son has no secrets from me. We've never lived apart, although he's now past his fiftieth year. I haven't the slightest idea of your business or of what brings you here, and, before going to disturb him, I would like to know ...'

She left the sentence unfinished, glancing from one to the other with a gracious smile.

'Your son is married, I believe?'

'He's been married twice.'

'Is his second wife at home?'

A shade of melancholy clouded her eyes, and Boissier began to cross and uncross his legs; this was not the sort of place he felt at home in.

'She's no longer with us, Chief-Inspector.'

She moved softly over to close the door, and returning, sat down in the corner of a sofa, keeping her back very straight, as young girls are taught to hold themselves in convent schools.

'I hope she hasn't done anything silly?' she asked in a low voice.

Then, as Maigret remained silent, she gave a sigh, resigned herself to begin once more:

'If it's anything to do with her, I was right to question you before disturbing my son. It is about her that you've come, isn't it?'

Did Maigret make a vague sign of assent? He was not aware of doing so. He was too intrigued by the atmosphere of this house, and even more by this woman, behind whose meekness he could sense an indomitable strength of will.

Everything about her was in good taste: her clothes, her bearing, and her voice. One might have expected to meet her in some château or, better still, in one of those enormous country houses that are like museums of a bygone age.

'After he became a widower, fifteen years ago, the thought of remarrying didn't enter my son's head for a long time.'

'He did remarry, two years ago, if I'm not mistaken?'

She showed no surprise at finding him so well-informed.

'He did, indeed. Two and a half years ago exactly. He married one of his patients, a woman also of a certain age. She was then forty-seven. Of Dutch origin, she lived alone in Paris. I won't live for ever, Chief-Inspector. As you see me now, I am seventy-eight.'

'You don't look it.'

'I know. My mother lived to the age of ninety-two, and my grandmother was killed in an accident at ninety-eight.'

'And your father?'

'He died young.'

She spoke as though this were of no importance, or rather as if men in general were doomed to die young.

'I almost encouraged Guillaume to marry again, by saying that thus he would not be left to live alone.'

'The marriage was unhappy?'

'I wouldn't say that. Not to begin with. I think that the trouble arose mainly from her being a foreigner. There are all sorts of little things that one cannot get used to. I don't quite know how to explain. Oh, yes. Food, for instance! A preference for this or that dish! Perhaps, too, when she married my son she imagined him to be wealthier than he actually is.'

'She'd no income of her own?'

'A certain competence. She was not badly off, but, with the rising cost of living ...'

'When did she die?'

The old woman's eyes opened wide.

'Die?'

'I'm sorry. I thought she was dead. You yourself speak of her in the past tense.'

She smiled.

'That's true. But not for the reason you imagine. She isn't dead; only for us it's as though she were, she's gone away.'

'After a quarrel?'

'Guillaume is not the kind of man who quarrels.'

'With you?'

'I am too old to quarrel now, Chief-Inspector. I've seen too much. I know life too well, and I let everybody ...'

'When did she leave the house?'

'Two days ago.'

'Did she tell you she was going?'

'My son and I knew that she would go in the end.'

'She had talked to you about it?'

'Often.'

'Did she give you any reasons?'

She did not reply at once, seemed to be pondering.

'Do you want me to tell you frankly what I think? If I hesitate, it's because I fear you may laugh at me. I don't like to discuss such things in front of men, but I suppose that a police officer is rather like a doctor or a priest.'

'You are a Roman Catholic, Madame Serre?'

'Yes. My daughter-in-law was a Protestant. That made no difference. You see, she was at the awkward age for a woman. We all, more or less, have to go through a few years during which we are not our normal selves. We get upset over trifles. We are apt to see things out of perspective.'

'I understand. That's what it was?'

'That and other things, probably. In the end, she dreamed only of her native Holland, spent all day writing to friends that she had kept up with over there.'

'Did your son ever go to Holland with her?'

'Never.'

'So she left on Tuesday?'

'She went on the nine-forty from the Gare du Nord.'

'The night-train?'

'Yes. She had spent the whole day packing.'

'Your son went with her to the station?'

'No.'

'Did she take a taxi?'

'She went to fetch one from the corner of the Boulevard Richard-Wallace.'

'She hasn't got in touch with you since?'

'No. I don't suppose she feels it necessary to write to us.'

'Was there any question of a divorce?'

'I've told you that we are Catholics. Moreover, my son has no wish to get married again. I still do not understand why the police have seen fit to call upon us.'

'I would like to ask you, Madame, exactly what happened here on Tuesday night. One moment. You haven't a maid, have you?'

'No, Chief-Inspector. Eugénie, our charwoman, comes every day from nine till five.'

'Is she here today?'

'You have come on her day off. She'll come in again tomorrow.'

'She lives in the neighbourhood?'

'She lives at Puteaux, on the other side of the Seine. Above an ironmonger's shop, directly opposite the bridge.'

'I suppose she helped your daughter-in-law to pack?'

'She brought the cases downstairs.'

'How many cases?'

'One trunk and two leather suit-cases precisely. Then there was a jewel-box and a dressing-case.'

'Eugénie left at five as usual?'

'She did, indeed. Please forgive me if I seem disconcerted, but this is the first time I've ever been cross-questioned like this and I must confess …'

'Did your son go out that evening?'

'What time of evening do you mean?'

'Let's say before dinner.'

'He went out for his usual stroll.'

'I suppose he went to have an *apéritif*?'

'He doesn't drink.'

'Never?'

'Nothing except a glass of wine and water at meal-times. Still less those horrible things called *apéritifs*.'

It seemed then that Boissier, who was sitting on his best behaviour in his arm-chair, sniffed the smell of aniseed which still clung to his moustache.

'We sat down to table as soon as he came in. He always takes the same stroll. It became a habit with him in the days when we had a dog that had to be exercised at set times and, I declare, it's become second nature to him.'

'You haven't a dog nowadays?'

'Not for four years. Not since Bibi died.'

'Or a cat?'

'My daughter-in-law loathed cats. You see! I spoke of her again in the past tense, and it's because we really do think of her as belonging to the past.'

'The three of you had dinner together?'

'Maria came down just as I was bringing in the soup.'

'There was no quarrelling?'

'None. Nobody spoke during the meal. I could tell that Guillaume, after all, was a little upset. At first sight, he seems cold, but really he's a terribly sensitive boy. When one has lived on terms of intimacy with someone for over two years ...'

Maigret and Boissier had not heard a thing. But she, the old lady, was sharp of hearing. She bent her head as though she were listening. It was a mistake, for Maigret understood, rose to his feet, and went and opened the door. A man, undoubtedly taller, broader, and heavier than the Chief-Inspector, stood there, slightly shame-faced, for he had plainly been eavesdropping for some time.

His mother had told the truth when she claimed that he'd been taking a siesta. His sparse hair, ruffled, clung to his forehead, and he'd pulled on trousers over his white shirt, with his collar still unbuttoned. He wore carpet slippers on his feet.

'Won't you come in, Monsieur Serre?' asked Maigret.

'I beg your pardon. I heard voices. I thought ...'

He spoke deliberately, turning his heavy, brooding stare upon each of them in turn.

'These gentlemen are police officers,' his mother explained, rising to her feet.

He didn't ask for any explanation, stared at them again, buttoned up his shirt.

'Madame Serre was telling us that your wife left the day before yesterday.'

This time he turned round to face the old lady, his brows together. His big frame was flaccid, like his face, but, unlike many fat men, he did not give an impression of agility. His complexion was very pale and sallow, tufts of dark hair sprouted from his nostrils, from his ears, and he had enormously bushy eyebrows.

'What exactly do these gentlemen want?' he asked, carefully spacing out the syllables.

'I don't know.'

And even Maigret felt at a loss. Boissier wondered how the Chief-Inspector was going to get out of the situation. These weren't the sort of people who could be put through the third degree.

'Actually, Monsieur Serre, the question of your wife merely cropped up in the course of conversation. Your mother told us that you were lying down, and we had a little talk while we were waiting for you. We're here, my colleague and myself' – the term 'colleague' gave Boissier so much pleasure! – 'simply because we've reason to believe that you have been the victim of an attempted burglary.'

Serre was not the sort of man who is unable to look others in the face. Far from it, he stared at Maigret as though attempting to read his innermost thoughts.

'What gave you that idea?'

'Sometimes we come into possession of confidential information.'

'You are speaking, I suppose, of police informers?'

'Let's put it like that.'

'I'm sorry, gentlemen.'

'Your house hasn't been burgled?'

'If it had been, I would have lost no time in lodging a complaint myself with the local police.'

He wasn't trying to be civil. Not once had he shown even the vestige of a smile.

35

'You are, however, the owner of a safe?'

'I believe that I'd be within my rights in refusing to answer you. I don't mind telling you, however, that I have got one.'

His mother was attempting to make signs to him, advising him, probably, not to be so ill-tempered.

He realized this and remained obdurate.

'If I'm not mistaken, it's a safe installed by Messrs Planchart about eighteen years ago.'

He remained unperturbed. He continued to stand, whilst Maigret and Boissier sat in semi-darkness, and Maigret saw that he had the same heavy jowl as the man in the portrait, the same eyebrows. The Chief-Inspector wondered whimsically what he'd look like with side-whiskers.

'I don't remember when I had it put in, nor is that anybody's business but mine.'

'I noticed, as we came in, that the front door is secured by a chain and a safety-lock.'

'So are lots of front doors.'

'You sleep on the first landing, your mother and yourself?'

Serre deliberately made no reply.

'Your study and surgery are on the ground floor?'

From a gesture on the part of the old lady, Maigret understood that these rooms led out of the drawing-room.

'Would you mind if I took a look round?'

He paused, opened his mouth, and Maigret felt certain it was to say no. His mother sensed this, too, for she intervened.

'Why not comply with these gentlemen's request? They will see for themselves that there has been no burglary.'

The man shrugged his shoulders, his expression as stubborn, as sullen, as ever, and he refrained from following them into the neighbouring rooms.

Madame Serre showed them first into a study as peaceful and old-fashioned as the drawing-room. Behind a black-leather-bottomed chair, stood a big safe, painted dark green, of a rather obsolete type. Boissier went up to it, smoothed the steel with a professional touch.

'You see that everything is in order,' said the old woman. 'You mustn't mind my son being in a bad temper, but ...'

She stopped as she saw the latter, framed in the doorway, fixing them with the same morose stare.

Then, waving a hand towards the bound volumes which filled the shelves, she went on, with a strained sprightliness:

'Don't be surprised to see mostly books on law. They're part of my husband's library, who was a solicitor.'

She opened one last door. And here the furnishings were more commonplace; it might have been any dental surgery, with a mechanical chair and the usual instruments. Up to half the height of the window, the panes were frosted.

On their way back through the study Boissier crossed to one of the windows, again felt with his fingers on it, then gave Maigret a significant nod.

'Has this window-pane been put in recently?' asked the latter in his turn.

It was the old woman who answered immediately:

'Four days ago. The window was open during the big thunderstorm which I'm sure you remember.'

'Did you call in the glazier?'

'No.'

'Who replaced the pane?'

'My son. He likes doing odd jobs. He always sees to any of our little household repairs.'

At which Guillaume Serre said with a touch of irritation:

'These gentlemen have no right to pester us, Mamma. Don't answer any more questions.'

She turned so that her back was towards him, and smiled at Maigret in a way that meant plainly:

'Don't mind him. I did warn you.'

She showed them to the front door, while her son remained standing in the centre of the drawing-room, and leaned forward to whisper:

37

'If you have anything to say to me, come and call when he isn't here.'

They were outside in the sunlight again, which made the clothes cling immediately to their skin. Once outside the gate – its faint creak was reminiscent of a convent gate – they caught sight, on the opposite pavement, of Ernestine's green hat as she sat at a table outside the café-restaurant.

Maigret halted. They could have turned left and avoided her. If they joined her, it would look almost as though they had to give her an account of themselves.

Perhaps out of a sense of decency, the Chief-Inspector growled: 'Shall we go and have one?'

With an inquiring expression, she watched them come towards her.

Chapter Three

'WHAT did you do today?' asked Madame Maigret, as they sat down to eat in front of the open window.

In the houses opposite also people could be seen eating, and, on every side, the same bright splashes of shirts showed where the men had taken off their jackets. Some of them, who'd finished dinner, were leaning on their elbows out of the window. Wireless music could be heard playing, babies crying, raised voices. A few concierges had brought their chairs out in front of their doorsteps.

'Nothing out of the way,' replied Maigret. 'A Dutch-woman who may have been murdered, but who's probably still alive somewhere.'

It was too early to talk about it. On the whole, he'd be-haved slackly. They'd sat about for a long time outside the little café in the Rue de la Ferme, Boissier, Ernestine, and himself, and of the three it was Ernestine who'd been the most worked up.

She took umbrage:

'He made out it wasn't true?'

The proprietor had brought them pints of beer.

'Actually he didn't say anything. It was his mother who did the talking. On his own, he'd have thrown us out.'

'He says there wasn't a corpse in the study?'

She'd obviously found out from the café owner about the residents in the house with the wrought-iron gate.

'Then why didn't he tell the police that somebody'd tried to burgle the place?'

'According to him, no one tried to burgle him.'

Of course she knew all about Sad Freddie's little ways.

'Wasn't there a pane missing in one of the windows?'

Boissier looked at Maigret, as if advising him to say no-thing, but the Chief-Inspector took no notice.

39

'A pane has been mended recently; it appears that it got broken four or five days ago, on the night of the storm.'

'He's lying.'

'Somebody's lying, certainly.'

'You think it's me?'

'I didn't say so. It might be Alfred.'

'Why should he have told me all that story on the phone?'

'Perhaps he didn't,' interposed Boissier, watching her narrowly.

'And what should I have made it up for? Is that what you think, too, Monsieur Maigret?'

'I don't think anything.'

He was smiling vaguely. He felt comfortable, almost blissful. The beer was cool, and in the shade it smelt almost like the country, perhaps because the Bois de Boulogne was close by.

A lazy afternoon. They'd drunk two pints apiece. Then, so as not to leave the girl stranded so far from the centre of Paris, they gave her a lift in their taxi and dropped her at the Châtelet.

'Ring me up directly you get a letter.'

He felt she was disappointed in him, that she'd imagined him otherwise. She must be telling herself that he'd got old, had become like the rest of them, and couldn't be much bothered with her case.

'D'you want me to put back my leave?' Boissier had suggested.

'I suppose your wife's done all the packing?'

'The bags are at the station already. We were due to go on the six-o'clock train tomorrow morning.'

'With your daughter?'

'Naturally.'

'Off you go.'

'Won't you be needing me?'

'You've trusted me with the file.'

Once alone in his office, he nearly dozed off in his chair.

The wasp was no longer there. The sun had moved round to the other side of the quay. Lucas had been off duty since noon. He called Janvier, who had been the first to take his leave, in June, because of a wedding in some branch of his family.

'Sit down. I've got a job for you. You've made out your report?'

'I've just this minute finished it.'

'Right! Take a note of this. First you've got to look up, at the Town Hall in Neuilly, the maiden name of a Dutch-woman who, two and a half years ago, married a man called Guillaume Serre, residing at 43b Rue de la Ferme.'

'Easy.'

'I dare say. She must have been living in Paris for some time. You must try to find out where, what she did, what relatives she had, how much money, etc ...'

'Right you are, Chief.'

'She's supposed to have left the house in the Rue de la Ferme on Tuesday, between eight and nine in the evening, and to have taken the night-train to Holland. She went to fetch a taxi herself from the corner of the Boulevard Richard-Wallace to take her luggage.'

Janvier was writing words in columns on a page of his notebook.

'That's all?'

'No. Get some help to save time. I want the people in the neighbourhood, tradesmen and so on, questioned about the Serres.'

'How many are there?'

'Mother and son. The mother's nearly eighty and the son's a dentist. Try to locate the taxi. Also make inquiries from the staff at the station and on the train.'

'Can I have transport?'

'You can.'

And that was about all he'd done that afternoon. He'd asked to be put through to the Belgian police, who had Sad Freddie's description but had not yet found him. He also had a long conversation with the passport inspector on the frontier at Jeumont. The latter had himself gone over the train which Alfred was thought to have taken, and didn't remember any passenger resembling the expert safe-cracker.

That meant nothing. He just had to wait. Maigret signed a few papers on behalf of the Chief, went to have a drink at the Brasserie Dauphine together with a colleague in the Records Office, and then back home by bus.

'What shall we do?' asked Madame Maigret, when the table had been cleared.

'Let's go for a stroll.'

Which meant that they'd amble along as far as the main boulevards to finish up sitting at a café terrace. The sun had set. The air was becoming cooler, though gusts of warm air still seemed to rise up from the paving-stones. The bay-windows of the *brasserie* were open, and a depleted orchestra played inside. Most of the customers sat there without speaking, like them, at their tables, watching the passers-by, and their faces melted more and more into the dusk. Then the electric-light made them look quite different.

Like the other couples, they turned back towards home, Madame Maigret's hand crooked in her husband's arm.

After that it was another day, as clear and sunny as the one before.

Instead of going straight to Headquarters, Maigret made a detour by the Quai de Jemmapes, identified the green-painted café, near the Saint-Martin Lock, with the sign 'Snacks served at all hours', and went in to lean against the counter.

'A white wine.'

Then he put the question. The Auvergnat who served him answered unhesitatingly:

'I don't know at what time exactly, but someone rang up. It was already daylight. My wife and I didn't get up, because, at that time, it couldn't have been for us. Ernestine went down. I heard her talking a long time.'

That was one thing at least she had not lied about.

'What time did Alfred go out, the night before?'

'Eleven, maybe? Maybe earlier. What I do remember is that he took his bike.'

A door led straight from the café into the passageway, from which a staircase mounted to the floors above. The wall of the staircase was whitewashed, as in the country. One could hear the racket made by a crane unloading gravel from a barge a little farther on.

Maigret knocked at a door, which half-opened; Ernestine appeared in her underclothes and merely said:

'It's you!'

Then she went at once to fetch her dressing-gown from the unmade bed, and slipped it on.

Did Maigret smile in memory of the Ernestine-that-used-to-be?

'You know, it's really a kindness,' she said frankly. 'I'm not a pretty sight these days.'

The window was open. There was a blood-red geranium. The bedspread was red, too. A door stood open into a little kitchen, out of which came a good smell of coffee.

He didn't quite know what he'd come for.

'There was nothing at the poste restante yesterday evening?'

She answered, worried:

'Nothing.'

'You don't think it odd that he hasn't written?'

'Perhaps he's just being canny. He must be surprised to see nothing in the papers. He probably thinks I'm being watched. I was just going to the post office.'

An old trunk lay in a corner.

'Those are his belongings?'

'His and mine. Between the two of us, we don't own much.'

Then, with an understanding look:

'Like to make a search? Of course! I know. It's your duty. You'll find a few tools, because he's got a spare set, also two old suits, some dresses, and a bit of linen.'

43

As she spoke, she was turning out the contents of the trunk on to the floor, opening the drawers of a dressing-table.

'I've been thinking it over. I've grasped what you were getting at yesterday. Of course somebody must have been lying. Either it's those people, the mother and her son, or it's Alfred, or it's me. You've no reason to believe any of us in particular.'

'Has Alfred no relatives in the country?'

'He's got no relatives anywhere now. He only knew his mother, and she's been dead twenty years.'

'You've never been anywhere together outside Paris?'

'Never farther than Corbeil.'

He couldn't be hiding out at Corbeil. It was too near. Maigret was beginning to think that he hadn't gone to Belgium either.

'There's no place he used to talk about, that he'd have liked to visit one day?'

'He always said the country, no special part. That summed it all up, to him.'

'Were you born in the country yourself?'

'Near Nevers, in a village called Saint-Martin-des-Prés.'

She took from a drawer a postcard that showed the village church, standing opposite a pond which served to water cattle.

'Did you show him this?'

She understood. Girls like Ernestine soon understand.

'I'd be surprised to find him there. He really was near the Gare du Nord when he phoned me.'

'How d'you know?'

'I found the bar, yesterday evening. It's in the Rue de Maubeuge, near a leather-goods shop. It's called the Bar du Levant. The owner remembers him because he was the first customer that day. He'd just lit the percolator when Alfred got there. Wouldn't you like a cup of coffee?'

He didn't like to refuse, but he'd just drunk white wine.

'No offence.'

He had some difficulty finding a taxi in those parts, eventually was driven to the Bar du Levant.

'A thin little chap, sad-looking, with eyes all red as if he'd been crying,' they told him.

Unquestionably Alfred Jussiaume, who often had red-rimmed eyes.

'He talked a long time at the phone, drank two coffees without sugar, and went off towards the station, looking round him as if he was scared of being followed. Has he done anything wrong?'

It was ten o'clock when Maigret at last climbed the staircase at Headquarters, where dust-motes still floated like a mist in the sunlight. Contrary to his usual custom, he didn't glance in through the glass partition of the waiting-room, and went past into the Duty Room, which was almost empty.

'Janvier not in yet?'

'He came about eight and went out again. He left a note on your desk.'

The note said:

The woman is called Maria Van Aerts. She is fifty-one and comes from Sneeck, in Friesland, Holland. I'm going to Neuilly, where she lived in a boarding-house, Rue de Longchamp. Haven't found the taxi yet. Vacher's looking after the station.

Joseph, the office-boy, opened the door.

'I didn't see you come in, Monsieur Maigret. A lady's been waiting for you half an hour.'

He held out an appointment-slip, on which old Madame Serre had inscribed her name in small, sharp handwriting.

'Shall I show her in?'

Maigret put on his jacket that he'd just taken off, went to open the window, filled his pipe, and sat down.

'Yes, show her in.'

He wondered what she would seem like outside the framework of her home, but, to his surprise, she didn't look out of place at all. She wasn't dressed in black, as on the

45

day before; she wore a frock with a white ground, on which dark patterns were traced. Her hat was not ludicrous. She moved forward with assurance.

'You were more or less expecting me to call, weren't you, Chief-Inspector?'

He had not been expecting it and refrained from telling her so.

'Do sit down, Madame.'

'Thank you.'

'The smoke doesn't worry you?'

'My son smokes cigars all day long. I was so upset yesterday at the way he received you! I tried to make signs to you not to persist, because I know him.'

She showed no nervousness, chose her words carefully, aimed at Maigret now and then a sort of conspiratorial smile.

'I think it is I who brought him up badly. You see, I had but the one child and, when my husband died, he was only seventeen years old. I spoilt him. Guillaume was the only man in the house. If you have any children ...'

Maigret looked at her to try to sum up her background and did not succeed. Something made him ask:

'Were you born in Paris?'

'In the house that you came to yesterday.'

It was a coincidence to find in one case two people born in Paris. Almost invariably, the people he dealt with were more or less directly connected with the provinces.

'And your husband?'

'His father, before him, used to be a solicitor in the Rue de Tocqueville, seventeenth *arrondissement*.'

That made three! To end up in the atmosphere, so absolutely provincial, of the house in the Rue de la Ferme!

'My son and myself have almost always lived alone together, and I suppose that is what has made him a little unsociable.'

'I understood that he'd been married before.'

'He was. His wife didn't live long.'

46

'How many years after their marriage did she die?'

She opened her mouth; he guessed that a sudden thought made her pause. He even had the impression of seeing a slight flush mount to her cheeks.

'Two years,' she said at last. 'That's curious, is it not? It only struck me just now. He lived for two years with Maria, as well.'

'Who was his first wife?'

'A person of very good family, Jeanne Devoisin, whom we met one summer at Dieppe, at the time when we used to go there every year.'

'Was she younger than he?'

'Let me see. He was thirty-two. She was more or less the same age. She was a widow.'

'Had she any children?'

'No. I don't think she had any relatives, except a sister living in Indo-China.'

'What did she die of?'

'A heart attack. She had a weak heart and spent most of her time under the care of doctors.'

She smiled again:

'I haven't told you yet why I am here. I nearly telephoned to you yesterday, when my son went out for his evening stroll, then I thought it would be more polite to come and call on you. I wish to apologize for Guillaume's attitude towards you and to say that his ill-humour was not directed at you personally. He has such a fierce temperament.'

'So I saw.'

'At the very idea that you could suspect him of a dishonest action ... He was like that even as a small boy ...'

'He lied to me?'

'I beg your pardon?'

The old lady's face expressed genuine surprise.

'Why should he have lied to you? I don't understand. You didn't really ask any questions. It's precisely to answer any which you should wish to put to me that I have come here. We have nothing to hide. I've no idea of the

47

circumstances that have led you to bother about us. It must be some misunderstanding, or some neighbour's spitefulness.'

'When was the window-pane broken?'

'I told you or my son told you, I can't remember now: during the thunderstorm last week, I was on the first floor and I hadn't had time to shut all the windows when I heard a crash of glass.'

'Was it in broad daylight?'

'It must have been six o'clock in the evening.'

'Which means the charwoman, Eugénie, was no longer there?'

'She leaves us at five, I think I explained that to you also. I haven't told my son that I was coming to see you. I thought that you might like, perhaps, to visit the house, and it would be easier when he's not there.'

'You mean during his late afternoon stroll?'

'Yes. You do understand that there's nothing to hide in our home, and that, if it weren't for Guillaume's nature, everything would have been cleared up yesterday.'

'You realize, Madame Serre, that you came here of your own free will?'

'Yes, of course.'

'And that it's you who want me to question you?'

She nodded her head in confirmation.

'We'll go over your movements again, then, from the last meal that you, your son, and your daughter-in-law took together. Your daughter-in-law's luggage was ready. In which part of the house was it?'

'In the corridor.'

'Who brought it down?'

'Eugénie brought down the suit-cases, and my son took charge of the trunk, too heavy for her.'

'Is it a very big trunk?'

'What they call a cabin-trunk. Before her marriage, Maria travelled a lot. She has lived in Italy and Egypt.'

'What did you have to eat?'

The question seemed both to amuse and surprise her.

'Let me see! As it's I who do the cooking, I should be able to remember. Vegetable soup, to start with. We always have vegetable soup, so good for the health. Then I did grilled mackerel and potato purée.'

'And the sweet?'

'A chocolate custard. Yes. My son has always adored chocolate custard.'

'No argument broke out at table? What time did the meal end?'

'About half-past seven. I put the dishes in the kitchen sink and went upstairs.'

'So you weren't present at the departure of your daughter-in-law.'

'I wasn't very anxious to be. Moments such as those are painful, and I prefer to avoid emotion. I said *au revoir* to her downstairs, in the drawing-room. I've nothing against her. Everybody's as they are made and ...'

'Where was your son during that time?'

'In his study, I think.'

'You've no idea whether he had a last conversation with his wife?'

'It's unlikely. She'd gone upstairs again. I heard her in her room, getting ready.'

'Your house is very solidly built, like most old houses. I suppose that, from the first floor, it's hard to hear sounds coming from downstairs?'

'Not for me,' she answered, pursing her lips.

'What d'you mean?'

'That I have keen hearing. Not even a floorboard can creak without my hearing it.'

'Who went to fetch the taxi?'

'Maria. I told you so yesterday.'

'Did she stay out long?'

'Fairly long. There's no rank near by, and one has to wait for a taxi to come cruising by.'

'Did you go to the window?'

She hesitated imperceptibly.

'Yes.'

'Who carried the trunk as far as the taxi?'

'The driver.'

'You don't know what company the cab belonged to?'

'How would I know that?'

'What colour was it?'

'Reddish-brown, with a coat-of-arms on the door.'

'Can you remember the driver?'

'Not very well. I think he was small and rather fat.'

'How was your daughter-in-law dressed?'

'She wore a mauve frock.'

'No coat?'

'She had it over her arm.'

'Was your son still in the study?'

'Yes.'

'What happened then? Did you go down?'

'No.'

'You didn't go to see your son?'

'It was he who came up.'

'Immediately?'

'Not long after the taxi drove away.'

'Was he upset?'

'He was as you have seen him. He's of a rather gloomy nature. I explained to you that he's really a highly sensitive man, likely to be affected by the smallest happenings.'

'Did he know that his wife was not coming back?'

'He suspected it.'

'She told him so?'

'Not exactly. She just hinted. She talked of the necessity to change her ideas, to see her own country again. Once over there, you understand ...'

'What did you do then?'

'I dressed my hair for the night.'

'Your son was in your room?'

'Yes.'

'He didn't leave the house?'

'No. Why?'

'Where does he garage his car?'

'A hundred yards away, where some old stables have been turned into private garages. Guillaume has hired one of them.'

'So he can take his car out and put it back in without being seen?'

'Why should he want to hide?'

'Did he go downstairs again?'

'I have no idea. I think so. I go to bed early, and he usually reads until eleven o'clock or midnight.'

'In the study?'

'Or in his room.'

'His room is near yours?'

'Next door. There's a bathroom in between us.'

'Did you hear him go to bed?'

'Certainly.'

'At what time?'

'I didn't put on the light.'

'You didn't hear any noise later?'

'None.'

'I suppose that you're the first down in the morning?'

'In summer I come down at half-past six.'

'Did you go round all the rooms?'

'I went first into the kitchen to put some water on to boil, then I opened the windows, because that's the time when the air is still cool.'

'You went into the study then?'

'Probably.'

'You don't remember doing so?'

'I almost certainly did.'

'The broken pane was already repaired?'

'I suppose so ... yes ...'

'Did you notice any disorder in the room?'

'None, except for some cigar ends, as always, in the ash-trays, and perhaps a book or two lying around. I don't know what all this means, Monsieur Maigret. As you see, I answer your questions frankly. I came especially to do so.'

'Because you were worried?'

'No. Because I was ashamed of the way Guillaume treated you. And also because I sense something mysterious behind your visit. Women aren't like men. In my husband's time, for instance, if there were a noise in the house at night, he never moved from his bed, and it was I who went to look. You understand? It's probably the same with your own wife. Really, it's in a way for the same reason that I'm here. You talked about burglary. You seemed preoccupied with the question of Maria.'

'You haven't had any news of her?'

'I don't expect to receive any. You're hiding certain facts and that makes me curious. It's the same with sounds in the night. I hold that mysteries don't exist, that one only has to look at things squarely for them to become perfectly simple.'

She was watching him, sure of herself, and Maigret had a slight feeling that she looked upon him as a child, as another Guillaume. She seemed to be saying:

'Tell me everything that's worrying you. Don't be frightened. You'll see that it'll all come right.'

He, too, looked her straight in the face.

'A man broke into your house that night.'

The old woman's eyes were incredulous, with a tinge of pity, as though he'd still believed in werewolves.

'What for?'

'To burgle the safe.'

'Did he do it?'

'He got into the house by cutting out a pane of glass to open the window.'

'The pane that was already broken in the thunderstorm? No doubt he put it back afterwards.'

She still refused to take what he was saying seriously.

'What did he take away?'

'He took nothing away, because at a certain moment his

52

electric torch lit up something that he hadn't expected to find in the room.'

She was smiling.

'What sort of thing?'

'The dead body of a middle-aged woman, which may have been that of your daughter-in-law.'

'He told you that?'

He looked at the white-gloved hands that didn't tremble.

'Why don't you ask this man to come and repeat his accusations to me?'

'He's not in Paris.'

'Can't you make him come here?'

Maigret preferred to make no reply. He wasn't too pleased with himself. He was beginning to wonder if he, too, were not falling under the influence of this woman who had the comforting serenity of a Mother Superior.

She didn't get up, didn't fidget, didn't show indignation either.

'I have no idea what it's all about and I won't ask you. Perhaps you have some good reason for believing in this man. He's a burglar, isn't he? Whilst I am merely an old woman of seventy-eight who never did anyone any harm.

'Allow me, now that I know where we are, to invite you cordially to come to our house. I will open every door for you, I will show you anything that you may wish to see. And my son, once he's acquainted with the facts, will not fail, in his turn, to answer your questions.

'When will you come, Monsieur Maigret?'

Now she had risen to her feet, still perfectly at ease, and there was nothing aggressive in her manner, just a slight touch of bitterness.

'Probably this afternoon. I don't know yet. Has your son used the car, these last few days?'

'You can ask him, if you like.'

'Is he at home now?'

'It's possible. He was there when I went out.'

'Eugénie as well?'

53

'She is certainly there.'

'Thank you.'

He showed her to the door. Just as they reached it, she turned round.

'I'd like to ask a favour,' she said gently. 'When I've gone, try for a moment to put yourself in my place, forgetting that you have spent your life in dealing with crime. Imagine that it's you who are suddenly being asked the questions you put to me, you who are being suspected of killing someone in cold blood.'

That was all. She only added:

'Until this afternoon, Monsieur Maigret.'

Once the door was closed, he stood for a full minute without moving by the doorway. Then he went to look out of the window, soon caught sight of the old lady walking with quick short steps, in full sunshine, towards the Pont Saint-Michel.

He picked up the telephone.

'Get me the police-station at Neuilly.'

He didn't ask to be put through to the Station Officer, but to a sergeant whom he knew.

'Vanneau? Maigret here. I'm well, thanks. Listen. It's a bit tricky. Jump in a car and get round to 43b Rue de la Ferme.'

'The dentist's place? Janvier, who came here yesterday evening, spoke to me about him. Something to do with a Dutchwoman, isn't it?'

'Never mind. Time's getting on. The chap's not easy to handle, and I can't ask for a warrant just now. You've got to act quickly, before his mother gets there.'

'Is she far away?'

'At the Pont Saint-Michel. I suppose she's going to take a cab.'

'What shall I do with the man?'

'Bring him in, on some excuse. Tell him whatever you like, that you need him as a witness ...'

'And then?'

'I'll be there. Just the time it takes to get downstairs and jump in a car.'

'Suppose the dentist's not at home?'

'You keep watch and grab him before he gets inside.'

'Bit irregular, eh?'

'Quite.'

As Vanneau was going to ring off, he added:

'Take somebody with you and put him to watch the stables that they've turned into garages in the same street. One of the garages is hired by the dentist.'

'Right you are.'

A moment later Maigret was hurrying down the stairs and climbing into one of the police-cars parked in the courtyard. As the car turned round towards the Pont Neuf, he thought he caught sight of Ernestine's green hat. He wasn't sure of it and preferred not to lose time. To tell the truth, he'd given way to a sudden fit of resentment against Lofty.

Once they'd crossed the Pont Neuf, he felt remorseful, but it was too late.

Couldn't be helped! She'd wait for him.

Chapter Four

THE police-station was on the ground floor of the Town Hall, an ugly square building that stood in the middle of a waste land, with sparse trees around and a dirty flag dangling. Maigret could have gone straight from outside into the Duty Rooms; so as not to come face to face with Guillaume Serre, he took a roundabout way through the draughty corridors, where he soon got lost.

Here, too, the slackness of summer held sway. Doors and windows were open, documents fluttered on tables in the empty rooms, while clerks in shirt-sleeves exchanged seaside gossip and an occasional tax-payer wandered disconsolately about in search of an endorsement or a signature.

Maigret finally managed to light upon a policeman who knew him by sight.

'Sergeant Vanneau?'

'Second on the left, third door along the passage.'

'Would you go and fetch him for me? There should be someone with him. Don't say my name out loud.'

A few moments later Vanneau joined him.

'Is he there?'

'Yes.'

'How did it go off?'

'Middling. I'd taken good care to bring along a police summons. I rang. A servant answered and I asked to see her master. I had to wait about a bit in the passage. Then the bloke came down, and I handed him the paper. He read it, looked at me without saying anything.

'"If you'd like to come with me, I've a car outside."

'He shrugged his shoulders, took a Panama hat down from the hall-stand, shoved it on his head, and followed me out.

'Now he's sitting on a chair. He still hasn't uttered a word.'

A minute or two later, Maigret went into Vanneau's office, found Serre there smoking a very black cigar. The Chief-Inspector took up a seat in the Sergeant's chair.

'I'm sorry to have troubled you, Monsieur Serre, but I'd like you to answer a few questions.'

As on the day before, the huge dentist surveyed him broodingly, and he had no trace of cordiality in his gloomy stare. Maigret, all of a sudden, realized what the man reminded him of: the sort of sultan that one used to see pictures of at one time. He had the girth, the manifest weight; in all probability the strength, too. For, despite his fat, he gave the impression of being very strong. He had also the disdainful calm of those pashas that are depicted on cigarette packets.

Instead of making some sign of agreement, uttering a polite commonplace, or even voicing a protest, Serre took a buff-coloured form from his pocket, cast his eye over it.

'I've been summoned here by the Police Superintendent of Neuilly,' he said. 'I look forward to hearing what this Superintendent requires from me.'

'Am I to understand you refuse to answer my questions?'

'Emphatically.'

Maigret paused. He'd seen all sorts, the mutinous, the pig-headed, the wilful, the wily, but none had ever answered him back with such unruffled determination.

'I suppose it's no good arguing?'

'Not in my opinion.'

'Or trying to point out that your attitude doesn't show you in a good light?'

This time the other merely sighed.

'Very well. Wait. The Superintendent will see you now.'

Maigret went in search of the latter, who did not at once understand what was expected of him, and only grudgingly agreed to play his part. His quarters were more comfortable, almost sumptuous in comparison with the rest of the offices, and there was a marble clock on the mantelpiece.

'Show Monsieur Serre in!' he told the man on duty.

He motioned him to a chair with a red velvet seat.

'Do sit down, Monsieur Serre. It's just a matter of a routine check-up, and I won't waste your time.'

The Superintendent consulted a form which had just been brought to him.

'You are, I believe, the owner of a motor vehicle registered under the number RS 8822 L?'

The dentist confirmed this with a nod. Maigret had gone over to sit on the window-sill and was watching him very thoughtfully.

'The vehicle in question is still in your possession?'

Another nod of assent.

'When was the last time you used it?'

'I believe I've the right to know the reason for this interrogation.'

The Superintendent shifted in his chair. He didn't at all like the task which Maigret had entrusted to him.

'Just suppose that your car had been involved in an accident ...'

'Has it been?'

'Suppose the number had been notified to us as that of a car which had knocked somebody down?'

'When?'

The police officer threw Maigret a reproachful look.

'Tuesday evening.'

'Where?'

'Near the Seine.'

'My car didn't leave the garage on Tuesday evening.'

'Somebody might have used it without your knowledge.'

'I doubt it. The garage is locked up.'

'You're prepared to swear that you didn't use the car on Tuesday evening, or later during the night?'

'Where are the witnesses to the accident?'

Once again the Superintendent looked anxiously to Maigret for support. The latter, realizing that this was leading nowhere motioned to him not to take it any farther.

'I've no further questions, Monsieur Serre. Thank you.'

The dentist rose, seemed for a moment to fill the room with his bulk, put on his Panama hat, and left the room, after turning to stare fixedly at Maigret.

'I did what I could. As you saw.'

'I saw.'

'Did you get any lead out of it?'

'Perhaps.'

'That's a man who'll make trouble for us. He's a stickler for his rights.'

'I know.'

It seemed almost as if Maigret was unconsciously imitating the dentist. He had the same sombre, heavy expression. He, in turn, made for the door.

'What's he supposed to have done, Maigret?'

'I don't know yet. It may be that he's killed his wife.'

He went to thank Vanneau, and found himself outside once more, where the police-car awaited him. Before climbing in, he had a drink at the bar on the corner and, catching sight of himself in the mirror, wondered what he'd look like wearing a Panama hat. Then he smiled wryly at the thought that it was, in a way, a case of two heavy-weights engaged in a fight.

He said to the driver:

'Go round by the Rue de la Ferme.'

Not far from 43b, they caught sight of Serre walking along the pavement with long, rather indolent strides. As some fat men do, he straddled slightly. He was still smoking his long cigar. As he passed the garage, he couldn't have failed to notice the plain-clothes man who was keeping a look-out there and had no means of taking cover.

Maigret was reluctant to stop the car at the house with the black wrought-iron gate. What good would it do? They probably wouldn't let him in.

Ernestine was waiting for him in the glass-panelled ante-room at Headquarters. He showed her into his office.

'Any news?' she asked him.

'Not a thing.'

He was in a bad temper. She didn't know that he rather liked feeling bad-tempered at the beginning of a difficult case.

'I had a card this morning. I brought it to you.'

She handed him a coloured postcard depicting the Town Hall at Le Havre. There was no inscription, no signature, nothing save Lofty's address, c/o poste restante.

'Alfred?'

'It's his handwriting.'

'He didn't get over to Belgium?'

'Doesn't look like it. He must have fought shy of the frontier.'

'D'you think he might try to get away by sea?'

'It isn't likely. He's never set foot on a boat. I'm going to ask you something, Monsieur Maigret, but you've got to give me a straight answer. Suppose he was to come back to Paris, what'd happen to him?'

'You want to know if he'd be detained?'

'Yes.'

'For attempted burglary?'

'Yes.'

'Nobody could detain him, because he wasn't caught red-handed, and, for another thing, Guillaume Serre hasn't laid a complaint, even denies that anybody broke into his house.'

'So they'd let him alone?'

'Unless he was lying and something quite different happened.'

'Can I promise him that?'

'Yes.'

'In that case, I'll put a notice in the Personal Column. He always takes the same paper, because of the crossword.'

She looked at him hard for a moment.

'You don't seem too sure about things.'

'What things?'

'The case. Yourself. I don't know. Did you see the dentist again?'

'Half an hour ago.'

'What did he say?'

'Nothing.'

She'd nothing more to say either and used the telephone ringing as an excuse to take her leave.

'What is it?' Maigret growled into the mouthpiece.

'It's me, Chief. Could I see you in your room?'

A few seconds later, Janvier came into the office briskly, obviously very pleased with himself.

'I've got plenty of leads. Shall I give 'em to you right away? You got a bit of time to spare?'

His enthusiasm was a little damped by the behaviour of Maigret, who'd just taken off his coat and was loosening his tie to set his thick neck free.

'First, I went to the boarding-house I told you about. It's a bit like the hotels on the left bank, with potted palms in the hall and old ladies sitting around in cane chairs. There aren't many guests much under fifty. Most of 'em are foreigners, Englishwomen, Swiss, and Americans, who go to museums and write endless letters.'

'Well?'

Maigret knew the kind of thing. It wasn't worth going on about.

'Maria Van Aerts lived there for a year. They remember her, because she made herself popular in the place. She seems to've been very gay and laughed a lot, shaking her great big bosom. She used to stuff herself with pastries, went to all the lectures at the Sorbonne.'

'That all?' said Maigret, meaning that he couldn't see what Janvier was so excited about.

'Nearly every day she used to write letters of eight to ten pages.'

The Chief-Inspector shrugged his shoulders, then examined the Sergeant with more interest in his eye. He had caught on.

'Always to the same woman, a school friend who lives in Amsterdam and whose name I got hold of. This friend came to see her once. They shared a room for three weeks. I've an idea that even when married Maria Serre kept on writing. The friend's called Gertrude Oosting, she's the wife of a brewer. It shouldn't be hard to find out her address.'

'Ring through to Amsterdam.'

'Will you be wanting the letters?'

'The recent ones, if possible.'

'That's what I thought. Brussels still hasn't any news of Sad Freddie.'

'He's in Le Havre.'

'Shall I phone Le Havre?'

'I'll do it myself. Who's free next door?'

'Torrence came back to duty this morning.'

'Send him to me.'

Another heavy-weight, who wouldn't pass unnoticed on the pavement of an empty street.

'You go and stick yourself down in Neuilly, Rue de la Ferme, facing 43b, a house with a garden and an iron gate in front. Don't bother to take cover. Far from it. If you see a chap come out, bigger and taller than you, follow him so that he can see you.'

'Anything else?'

'Arrange to be relieved part of the night. There's a man from Neuilly on duty a bit farther on, opposite the garage.'

'What if the bloke goes off by car?'

'Take one of ours and park it along the kerb.'

He hadn't the energy to go home for lunch. It was hotter than the day before. There was thunder in the air. Most men were walking about with their jackets over their arms, and urchins were swimming in the Seine.

He went to have a bite at the Brasserie Dauphine, first having drunk, as if as a challenge, a couple of Pernods.

Then he went to see Moers of the Technical Branch, under the overheated roof of the Palais de Justice.

'Let's say about eleven in the evening. Bring the things you need. Take someone with you.'

'Yes, Chief.'

He'd sent out a call to the police at Le Havre. Had Sad Freddie taken a train at the Gare du Nord, after all, to Lille, for instance; or, having telephoned Ernestine, had he made a dash straight away for the Gare Saint-Lazare?

He must have gone to ground in some cheap lodging, or be wandering from bar to bar, drinking baby bottles of Vichy water, unless he was trying to stow away on board some ship. Was it as hot in Le Havre as it was in Paris?

They still hadn't found the taxi that was supposed to have picked up Maria Serre and her luggage. The staff at the Gare du Nord had no recollection of her.

Opening the paper, about three o'clock, Maigret read Ernestine's message in the Personal Column:

> Alfred. Return Paris. No danger.
> All arranged. Tine.

At half-past four he found himself still in his chair, the newspaper on his knee. He hadn't turned the page. He'd gone to sleep, and his mouth felt sticky, his back cricked.

None of the squad cars were in the courtyard and he had to take a taxi from the end of the quay.

'Rue de la Ferme, in Neuilly. I'll show you where to stop.'

He nearly dozed off again. It was five to five when he stopped the cab opposite the already familiar café. There was no one at the tables outside. Farther on the burly shape of Torrence could be seen, pacing up and down in the shade. He paid the driver, sat down with a sigh of relief.

'What can I get you, Monsieur Maigret?'

Beer of course! He had such a thirst he could have swallowed five or six pints at a gulp.

'He hasn't been in again?'

'The dentist? No. I saw his mother, this morning, going down towards the Boulevard Richard-Wallace.'

The wrought-iron gate creaked. A wiry little woman started to walk along the opposite pavement and Maigret settled for his drink, caught her up just as she reached the edge of the Bois de Boulogne.

'Madame Eugénie?'

'What d'you want?'

The Neuilly household wasn't conspicuous for its affability.

'A little chat with you.'

'I've no time to chat. There's all the housework to do when I get home.'

'I'm a police officer.'

'That makes no odds.'

'I'd like to ask you a few questions.'

'Do I have to answer?'

'It would certainly be better to.'

'I don't like policemen.'

'You're not obliged to. D'you like your employers?'

'They stink.'

'Old Madame Serre as well?'

'She's a bitch.'

They were standing by a bus stop. Maigret raised his arm to stop a cruising taxi.

'I'm going to take you home.'

'I don't care all that much for being seen with a copper, but I suppose it's worth it.'

She climbed into the cab with dignity.

'What have you got against them?'

'What about you? Why are you sticking your nose into their business?'

'Young Madame Serre has gone away?'

'Young?' she said ironically.

'Let's say the daughter-in-law.'

'She's gone, yes. Good riddance.'

'Was she a bitch, too?'

'No.'

'You didn't like her?'

'She was always digging into the larder, and when it came to lunch-time, I couldn't find half what I'd got ready.'

'When did she go?'

'Tuesday.'

They were crossing the Pont de Puteaux. Eugénie tapped on the glass.

'Here we are,' she said. 'D'you need me any more?'

'Could I come up with you for a moment?'

They were on a crowded square, and the charwoman made towards an alleyway, to the right of a shop, began to climb a staircase that smelt of slops.

'If only you could tell them to leave my son alone.'

'Tell whom?'

'The other coppers. The ones from hereabouts. They never stop making trouble for him.'

'What does he do?'

'He works.'

'Doing what?'

'How should I know? Can't be helped if the housework isn't done for you. I can't clean up after others all day long and do my own as well.'

She went to open the window, for a strong, stuffy smell hung about, but it wasn't untidy and, except for a bed in one corner, the sort of drawing-cum-dining-room was almost dainty.

'What's all the to-do?' she asked, taking off her hat.

'Maria Serre can't be found.'

'Course not, as she's in Holland.'

'They can't find her in Holland either.'

'Why do they want to find her?'

'We've reason to believe that she's been murdered.'

A tiny spark kindled in Eugénie's brown eyes.

'Why don't you arrest them?'

'We haven't any proof yet.'

'And you're counting on me to get you some?'

She put some water to heat on the gas, came over to Maigret again.

'What happened on Tuesday?'

'She spent all day packing.'

'Wait a moment. She'd been married two and a half years, hadn't she? I suppose she had a good many things of her own.'

'She'd at least thirty dresses and as many pairs of shoes.'

'Was she smart?'

'She never threw anything out. Some of the dresses dated back ten years. She didn't wear them, but she wouldn't have given them away for all the money in the world.'

'Mean?'

'Aren't all rich people mean?'

'I was told that all she took with her was a trunk and two suit-cases.'

'That's right. The rest went a week before.'

'You mean she sent other trunks away?'

'Trunks, packing-cases, cardboard boxes. A removal van came to fetch the lot, Thursday or Friday last.'

'Did you look at the labels?'

'I don't remember the exact address, but the stuff was booked for Amsterdam.'

'Did your employer know?'

'Of course he did.'

'So her departure had been decided on for some time?'

'Since her last attack. After each attack she'd talk of going back to her own country.'

'What kind of attacks?'

'Heart, so she said.'

'She'd a weak heart?'

'Seems like it.'

'Did a doctor come and see her?'

'Doctor Dubuc.'

'Did she take any medicine?'

'After each meal. They all did. The other two still do, and

66

they've each a little bottle of pills or drops beside their plate.'

'What's wrong with Guillaume Serre?'

'I don't know.'

'And his mother?'

'Rich people always have something wrong with them.'

'Did they get on well?'

'Sometimes they didn't speak to each other for weeks.'

'Maria Serre wrote a lot of letters?'

'Nearly from morning till night.'

'Did you ever happen to take them to the post?'

'Often. They were always to the same person, a woman with a funny name who lives in Amsterdam.'

'Are the Serres well off?'

'I reckon so.'

'What about Maria?'

'Sure. Otherwise he wouldn't have married her.'

'Did you work for them when they got married?'

'No.'

'You don't know who did the housework at that time?'

'They're always changing their daily help. It's my last week now. Soon as anybody begins to know the form, they pack in.'

'Why?'

'How would you like to see the lumps of sugar counted in the sugar-bowl and have a half-rotten apple picked out for your sweet?'

'Old Madame Serre?'

'Yes. Just because at her age she works all day, which is her own funeral, she's on to you like a shot if you're unlucky enough to be caught sitting down for a moment.'

'Does she tell you off?'

'She's never told me off. I'd like to see her! It's far worse. She's only too polite, she looks at you in a down-hearted sort of way as if it made her sad to see you.'

'Did anything strike you when you came to work on Wednesday morning?'

'No.'

'You didn't notice if a window had been broken during the night, or whether there was fresh putty round one of the panes?'

She nodded.

'You've got the wrong day.'

'Which day was it?'

'Two or three days before, when we had that big thunderstorm.'

'You're sure of that?'

'Certain. I even had to polish the floor of the study because the rain had come into the room.'

'Who put in the pane?'

'Monsieur Guillaume.'

'He went to buy it himself?'

'Yes. He brought back the putty. It was about ten o'clock in the morning. He had to go to the ironmonger's in the Rue de Longchamp. They never have a workman in if they can do without one, and Monsieur Guillaume unstops all the drains himself.'

'You're certain about the date?'

'Absolutely.'

'Thank you very much.'

Maigret had no further business there. There was really nothing more for him to do at the Rue de la Ferme either. Unless, of course, Eugénie was merely repeating a piece that she'd been taught to say and, in that case, she was a better liar than most.

'You don't think they've killed her?'

He didn't answer, went on towards the door.

'Because of the window-pane?'

There was a slight hesitation in her tone.

'Does the window have to be broken on the day you said?'

'Why? Do you want to see them go to jail?'

'Nothing I'd like better. But now that I've told the truth …'

She regretted it. For two pins she'd have gone back on her statement.

'You could always go and ask at the ironmonger's where he bought the glass and the putty.'

'Thank you for the tip.'

He stood for a moment in front of the shop outside, which happened in fact to be an ironmonger's. But it wasn't the right one. He waited for a taxi.

'Rue de la Ferme.'

There was no point in leaving Torrence and the plain-clothes man from Neuilly to kick their heels on the pavement any longer. The recollection of Ernestine playing her little joke in the Rue de la Lune came back to him, and he didn't find it at all funny, began to think about her. For it was she who'd started him off on this business. He'd been a fool to rush intó it. Only this morning, in the Police Superintendent's office, he'd made a proper ass of himself.

His pipe tasted foul. He crossed and uncrossed his legs. The partition was open between himself and the driver.

'Go round by the Rue de Longchamp. If the ironmonger's is still open, stop there for a moment.'

It was a toss-up. This would be his last throw. If the ironmonger's was closed, he wouldn't bother to come back, Ernestine and Sad Freddie notwithstanding. Anyway, what proof was there that Alfred had ever really broken into the house in the Rue de la Ferme?

He'd gone off on his bike from the Quai de Jemmapes, agreed, and at daybreak he'd telephoned his wife. But nobody knew what they'd said to each other.

'It's open!'

Of course, the ironmonger's, where the hardware department could be seen inside. A tall youth in a grey smock came to meet Maigret between the galvanized tin pails and the brooms.

'Do you sell sheet glass?'

'Yes, sir.'

'And putty?'

'Certainly. Have you brought the measurements?'

'It's not for myself. Do you know Monsieur Serre?'

'The dentist? Yes, sir.'

'Is he a customer of yours?'

'He's got an account here.'

'Have you seen him recently?'

'*I* haven't, because I only got back from my holiday day before yesterday. He might have come in while I was away. I can easily tell you by looking up the book.'

The salesman didn't ask the reason why, but dived into the semi-darkness of the shop, opened a ledger that lay on a tall, raised desk.

'He bought a sheet of window-glass last week.'

'Could you tell me which day?'

'Friday.'

The thunderstorm had occurred on Thursday night. Eugénie had been right, and old Madame Serre as well!

'He bought half a pound of putty, too.'

'Thank you.'

It hung by a thread, by an unthinking gesture on the part of the young man in the grey smock who wouldn't be long in shutting up shop. He was turning over the entries in the ledger, more or less for form's sake. He said:

'He came back again this week.'

'What!'

'Wednesday. He bought a pane of the same size, forty-two by sixty-five, and another half-pound of putty.'

'You're sure?'

'I can even tell you that he was in early, because it's the first sale made that day.'

'What time d'you open?'

An important point, since, according to Eugénie, who started work at nine, all the window-panes had been in good repair on Wednesday morning.

'Well, we get in at nine, but the boss comes down at eight to open the shop.'

'Thanks, old chap. You're a bright lad.'

The bright lad must have wondered for some time afterwards why this man, who had looked so depressed when he came in, now seemed to be in such high spirits.

'I suppose there's no danger of anyone destroying the pages in this ledger?'

'Why would anybody do that?'

'Why, indeed! All the same, I advise you to keep a look out. I'll send someone round tomorrow morning to photostat them.'

He took a card from his pocket, handed it to the young man, who read with astonishment:

Chief-Divisional-Inspector Maigret
Central Police Headquarters
Paris

'Where to now?' asked the driver.

'Pull up for a moment in the Rue de la Ferme. You'll see a little café on your left ...'

This deserved a pint of beer. He nearly called Torrence and the plain-clothes man to have one with him, but finally merely asked the driver in.

'What'll you have?'

'Mine's a white wine and Vichy.'

The street was gilded by the sun. They could hear the breeze rustling through the big trees in the Bois de Boulogne.

There was a black wrought-iron gate farther up the road, a square of greensward, a house as serene and well-ordered as a convent.

Somewhere in this house there lived an old woman like a Mother Superior and a sort of sultan with whom Maigret had a score to settle.

It was good to be alive.

Chapter Five

THE rest of the day went as follows. First of all, Maigret drank two pints of beer with the taxi-driver, who had only the one white wine and Vichy water himself. By that time it was beginning to get cooler and, as he climbed back into the cab, he'd the notion of driving round to the boarding-house that Maria Van Aerts had stayed in for a year.

There was nothing in particular for him to do there. He was simply following his habit of nosing round people's homes in order to understand them better.

The walls were cream-coloured. Everything was creamy, luscious, as in a dairy, and the proprietress with her floury face looked like a cake with too much icing on it.

'What a lovely person, Monsieur Maigret! And what a wonderful companion she must have made for her husband! She wanted to get married so much.'

'You mean she was looking for a husband?'

'Don't all young girls dream of a bridegroom?'

'She was about forty-eight when she lived here, if I'm not mistaken?'

'But she was still so young at heart! Anything could make her laugh. Would you believe it, she loved to play practical jokes on her fellow-guests. Near the Madeleine, there's a shop I'd never noticed before I found out about it through her, that sells all sorts of joke-novelties, mechanical mice, spoons that melt in the coffee, gadgets that you slide under the table-cloth to lift someone's plate up all of a sudden while they're eating, glasses that you can't drink from, and I don't know what all! Well, she was one of its best customers! A very cultured woman, all the same, who'd been to every museum in Europe and used to spend whole days at the Louvre.'

'Did she introduce you to her prospective husband?'

'No. She was secretive by nature. Perhaps she didn't like to bring him here, for fear that some of the others might be envious. He was a man of very imposing presence, who looked like a diplomat, I believe.'

'Aha!'

'He's a dentist, she told me, but only sees a few patients, by appointment. He belongs to a very rich family.'

'And Mademoiselle Van Aerts herself?'

'Her father left her a good deal of money.'

'Tell me, was she mean?'

'Oh, you've heard about that? She was certainly thrifty. For instance, when she had to go into town, she'd wait until one of the other guests was going too so that they could share the taxi. Every week she'd argue over her bill.'

'Do you know how she came to meet Monsieur Serre?'

'I don't think it was through the matrimonial advertisement.'

'She put an advertisement in the papers?'

'Not in earnest. She didn't believe in it. More for fun really. I don't remember the exact wording, but she said that a distinguished lady, foreign, wealthy, wished to meet gentleman of similar circumstances, with a view to marriage. She had hundreds of replies. She used to make dates with the suitors at the Louvre, sometimes in one gallery, sometimes in another, and they had to carry a certain book in their hand, or wear a button-hole.'

There were other women like her, from England, Sweden, or America, sitting in the wicker arm-chairs of the lounge, from which the smooth hum of the electric fans could be heard.

'I hope she hasn't come to any harm?'

It was about seven o'clock when Maigret got out of the taxi at the Quai des Orfèvres. From the shady side of the street he'd caught sight of Janvier coming along, with a preoccupied expression, a parcel under his arm, and he'd waited to climb the stairs with him.

'How's things, Janvier, my boy?'

'All right, Chief.'

'What have you got there?'

'My dinner.'

Janvier didn't grumble, but he had a martyred look.

'Why don't you go home?'

'Because of that woman Gertrude, blast her.'

The offices were almost empty, swept by draughts, for a breeze had just got up and all the windows in the building were still open.

'I managed to track down Gertrude Oosting in Amsterdam. Or rather, I got her maid on the phone. I had to dig up a chap waiting for an identity-card in the Aliens Section, who was willing to interpret, because the maid doesn't speak a word of French, and then call her back.

'As luck would have it, the good lady Oosting had gone out with her husband at four in the afternoon. There's some open-air concert on today, over there, with a fancy-dress parade, and after that the Oostings are having dinner with friends, the maid doesn't know where. She's no idea when they'll be back either, and she'd been told to put the children to bed.

'And, talking of children ...'

'What?'

'Nothing, Chief.'

'Come on, out with it!'

'Doesn't matter. Only that the wife's a bit disappointed. It's our eldest's boy's birthday. She'd got a special little dinner ready. Never mind.'

'Did you find out from the maid if Gertrude Oosting can speak French?'

'She can.'

'Go on home.'

'What?'

'I told you to go home. Leave me those sandwiches, and I'll stay on here.'

'Madame Maigret won't like that.'

74

Janvier needed a bit of pressure, but finally went rushing off to catch his train to the suburbs.

Maigret had eaten alone in his office, had gone down for a chat with Moers in the laboratory afterwards. Moers had not left until after nine, when darkness had completely fallen.

'Sure you know what to do?'

'Yes, Chief.'

He took a photographer with him, and masses of equipment. It wasn't strictly legal, but, ever since Guillaume Serre had bought two window-panes and not one, that no longer mattered.

'Get me Amsterdam, please ...'

At the other end the maid gabbled something and he understood her to mean that Madame Oosting still hadn't come in.

Then he called up his wife.

'You wouldn't mind coming down to have a drink at the Brasserie Dauphine? I've probably got another hour or so to fill in here. Take a cab.'

It wasn't a bad evening. The two of them were as comfortable as outside a café on the main boulevards, except that their view was blocked by the tall pale flight of steps leading to the Palais de Justice.

They ought to have got to work by now, in the Rue de la Ferme. Maigret had given them instructions to wait until the Serres had gone to bed. Torrence was to mount guard in front of the house to prevent the others from being taken unawares while they broke into the garage, which couldn't be overlooked from the house, and gave the car a thorough overhaul. Moers and the photographer would take care of that. Everything would be gone into: fingerprints, samples of dust for analysis, the whole works.

'You look pleased with yourself.'

'I can't complain.'

He wasn't prepared to admit that, a few hours earlier, he was far from being in such a good mood, and now he began to have short drinks, while Madame Maigret stuck to barley-water.

He left her twice to go back and call Amsterdam from the office. Not until half-past eleven did he hear a voice which was not the maid's and which answered him in French:

'I can't hear you very well.'

'I said, I'm calling from Paris.'

'Oh! Paris!'

She'd a strong accent, which nevertheless was not unattractive.

'Police Headquarters.'

'Police?'

'Yes. I'm telephoning with reference to your friend Maria. You know Maria Serre, whose maiden name was Van Aerts, don't you?'

'Where is she?'

'I don't know. That's just what I'm asking you. She often wrote to you?'

'Yes, often. I was supposed to meet her at the station, Wednesday morning.'

'Did you go to meet her?'

'Yes.'

'Did she come?'

'No.'

'Had she wired or telephoned you that she couldn't keep the appointment?'

'No. I'm worried.'

'Your friend has disappeared.'

'What do you mean?'

'What did she tell you in her letters?'

'Lots of things.'

She began to speak in her own language to someone, probably her husband, who was evidently standing beside her.

'Do you suppose Maria is dead?'

'It could be. Did she ever write to you that she was unhappy?'

'She was distressed.'

'Why?'

'She didn't like the old lady.'

'Her mother-in-law?'

'Yes.'

'What about her husband?'

'It appears that he wasn't a man, but just an overgrown schoolboy who was terrified of his mother.'

'How long ago did she write you that?'

'Almost as soon as she got married. A few weeks after.'

'She already talked about leaving him?'

'Not then. After about a year or so.'

'And recently?'

'She'd made up her mind. She asked me to find her a flat in Amsterdam, near ours.'

'Did you find one for her?'

'Yes. And a maid.'

'So it was all arranged?'

'Yes. I was at the station.'

'Have you any objection to sending me copies of your friend's letters? Did you keep them?'

'I have kept all the letters, but it would be hard work to copy them, as they are very long. I can send you the ones that matter. You're sure something's happened to her?'

'I'm convinced of it.'

'Somebody's killed her?'

'Possibly.'

'Her husband?'

'I don't know. Listen, Madame Oosting, you could do me a great favour. Has your husband got a car?'

'Of course.'

'It would be kind of you to drive to Central Police Head-quarters, which is open all night. Tell the Duty Officer that you were expecting your friend Maria. Show him her last letter. Then tell him you're very worried and that you'd like the matter gone into.'

'Should I mention your name?'

77

'It doesn't matter either way. What you must do is to insist upon an investigation.'

'I will do so.'

'Thank you. Don't forget the letters that you promised to send me.'

He rang Amsterdam again almost at once, asking this time for the number of Central Police Headquarters.

'In a few minutes, a Madame Oosting will be coming to see you about the disappearance of her friend, Madame Serre, *née* Van Aerts.'

'Did she disappear in Holland?'

'No, in Paris. In order to take action, I need an official complaint. Directly you've taken down her statement, I'd like you to send me a wire asking us to make inquiries.'

This took a bit of time. The Duty Officer at the other end couldn't understand how Maigret, in Paris, could have known that Madame Oosting was coming along.

'I'll tell you that later. All I must have is your wire. Send it priority. I should get it in less than half an hour.'

He went back to join Madame Maigret, who'd begun to get bored sitting about outside the *brasserie*.

'Have you done?'

'Not yet. I'll have one drink, and then we'll be off.'

'Home?'

'To the office.'

That always impressed her. She'd only rarely been within the walls of Headquarters, and didn't know how to behave there.

'You look as if you were having fun. One'd think you were playing a joke on somebody.'

'I am in a way.'

'On whom?'

'A fellow who looks like a sultan, a diplomat, and a schoolboy.'

'I don't understand.'

'Naturally not!'

He wasn't often in such high spirits. How many Calvados

had he drunk? Four? Five? This time, before going back to the office, he swallowed a pint and took his wife's arm before crossing the couple of hundred yards of the quay to reach Police Headquarters.

'I only ask one thing: don't start telling me again that everything's covered in dust and that the offices need a good clean-out!'

On the telephone:

'Any telegrams come through for me?'

'Nothing, Chief-Inspector.'

Ten minutes later the whole squad, with the exception of Torrence, was back from the Rue de la Ferme.

'Did it go off all right? No hitches?'

'No hitches. Nobody disturbed us. Torrence insisted we should wait until the lights had all gone out in the house, and Guillaume Serre hung about for a long time before going to bed.'

'The car?'

Vacher, who'd nothing more to do, asked if he could go home. Moers and the photographer stayed behind. Madame Maigret, sitting on a chair as if paying a visit, assumed the abstracted expression of one who is not listening.

'We went over every bit of the car, which doesn't seem to have been taken out for two or three days. The petrol tank's about half-full. There are no signs of a struggle inside. In the boot, I found two or three more or less recent scratches.'

'As if a large heavy piece of luggage had been stowed in it?'

'That could be.'

'A trunk, for instance?'

'A trunk or a packing-case.'

'Were there any blood-stains inside?'

'No. Nor any loose hairs either. I thought of that. We took a flashlight along, and there's a power point in the garage. Emile is going to make enlargements of the photos.'

'I'm getting on to it right now,' the photographer said. 'If you could wait just twenty minutes ...'

79

'I'll wait. Did it look to you, Moers, as if the car had been cleaned lately?'

'Not on the outside. It hadn't been washed down by a garage. But it looked as if the inside had been carefully brushed. They must have even taken up the mat to be beaten, because I'd a job to find any dust in it. All the same, I've got several specimens for laboratory tests.'

'Was there a brush in the garage?'

'No. I looked. They must have taken it away.'

'So, except for the scratches ...'

'Nothing out of the way. Can I go now?'

They were left alone, Madame Maigret and he, in the office.

'Aren't you sleepy?'

She said no. She'd her own special way of looking at the surroundings in which her husband had spent most of his life, of which she knew so little.

'Is it always like this?'

'What?'

'A case. When you don't come home.'

She must have thought it was easy, quiet work, more like a kind of game.

'Just depends.'

'Has there been a murder?'

'More than likely.'

'D'you know who did it?'

She turned her head away as he smiled at her. Then she asked:

'Does he know that you suspect him?'

He nodded.

'D'you suppose he's asleep?'

She added after a moment, with a slight shiver:

'It must be awful.'

'I don't suppose it was fun for the poor woman either.'

'I know. But probably that was quicker, don't you think?'

'Maybe.'

The telegram from the Dutch police came through on the

phone, with a confirmatory copy promised for the next morning.

'Now then! We can go home.'

'I thought you were waiting for the photographs.'

He smiled once more. Really, she'd have liked to find out. She didn't feel now like going back to bed.

'They won't tell us anything.'

'Don't you think so?'

'I'm sure of it. Moers' laboratory tests won't either.'

'Why not? Because the murderer was too careful?'

He did not reply, put out the light, and led his wife into the passage, where the cleaners were already at work.

'That you, Monsieur Maigret?'

He looked at the alarm clock, which said half-past eight. His wife had let him sleep on. He recognized Ernestine's voice.

'Did I wake you up?'

He preferred not to admit it.

'I'm at the post office. There's another card for me.'

'From Le Havre?'

'From Rouen. He doesn't say anything, still hasn't answered my advertisement. Nothing except my address at the poste restante, same as yesterday.'

There was a pause. Then she asked:

'You heard anything?'

'Yes.'

'What?'

'Something to do with window-panes.'

'Good?'

'Just depends for whom.'

'For us?'

'It may do Alfred and you some good.'

'You don't still think I've been telling lies?'

'Not at the moment.'

At Headquarters he picked Janvier to go with him, and the latter took the wheel of the little black police-car.

'Rue de la Ferme.'

With the telegram in his pocket, he made the car stop outside the wrought-iron gate, through which the two of them passed looking their most official. Maigret rang. A window curtain moved on the first floor, where the shutters were not yet closed. It was Eugénie, in down-at-heel slippers, who came to the door, wiping her wet hands on her apron.

'Good morning, Eugénie. Monsieur Serre is at home and I'd like a word with him.'

Somebody leant over the banisters. The old woman's voice said:

'Show the gentlemen into the drawing-room, Eugénie.'

It was the first time that Janvier had been in the house, and he was impressed. They heard footsteps coming and going overhead. Then the door opened abruptly and the huge bulk of Guillaume Serre almost filled the entrance.

He was as self-possessed as on the day before, stared at them with the same calm insolence.

'Have you a warrant?' he asked, his lip twitching slightly.

Maigret deliberately took some time taking his wallet from his pocket, opening it, finding a document, which he handed over politely.

'Here you are, Monsieur Serre.'

The man wasn't prepared for this. He read through the form, took it over to the window to decipher the signature, while Maigret was saying:

'As you see, it's a search warrant. Inquiries are being instituted into the disappearance of Madame Maria Serre, *née* Van Aerts, on a complaint lodged by Madame Gertrude Oosting, of Amsterdam.'

The old lady had entered on these last words.

'What is it, Guillaume?'

'Nothing, Mamma,' he told her in a curiously gentle voice. 'These gentlemen, I believe, would like to search the house. Go up to your room.'

She wavered, looked at Maigret as if to ask his advice.

'You'll keep your temper, Guillaume?'

'Of course, Mamma. Please leave us, I beg of you.'

Things weren't going exactly as Maigret had foreseen, and the Chief-Inspector frowned.

'I expect,' he said, when the old lady had reluctantly moved away, 'you'll want to consult your lawyer? I'll probably have a few questions to ask you later on.'

'I don't need a lawyer. Now that you have a warrant, I cannot object to your presence here. That's that.'

The shutters on the ground floor were closed. Until now they'd been in semi-darkness. Serre walked towards the nearest window.

'No doubt you'd prefer more light upon the scene?'

He spoke in a flat voice, and if any expression at all could be read into his tone, it was a degree of contempt.

'Do your duty, gentlemen.'

It came almost as a shock to see the drawing-room in full daylight. Serre went into his study next door, where he also opened the shutters, then into the surgery.

'When you wish to go up to the first floor, please let me know.'

Janvier was glancing in bewilderment at his Chief. The latter wasn't quite so buoyant as he'd been that morning or the night before. He seemed to be worried.

'May I use your telephone, Monsieur Serre?' he asked with the same cold courtesy the other had shown him.

'You have every right to.'

He dialled the number of Headquarters. Moers had made a verbal report that morning which, as the Chief-Inspector had expected, was more or less negative. The particles of dust had been analysed with no result. Or rather, almost none. Moers had only managed to scrape up, from the front of the car, by the driving-seat, a minute quantity of powdered brick.

'Give me the laboratory. That you, Moers? Can you come along to the Rue de la Ferme with your men and equipment?'

He was watching Serre, who, engaged in lighting a long black cigar, didn't bat an eyelid.

'All the lot, eh? No, there's no body. I'll be here.'

Then turning to Janvier:

'You can get started.'

'On this room?'

'On any one you like.'

Guillaume Serre followed them up step by step and watched what they were doing without a murmur. He wore no tie and had slipped on a black alpaca jacket over his white shirt.

While Janvier was searching the drawers of the desk, Maigret himself was going through the dentist's private files and making entries in his large notebook.

Really, it had begun to border on farce. He'd have been hard put to it to say precisely what he was looking for. What it amounted to in the end was seeing whether, at any given moment, in any particular part of the house, Serre would show any sign of uneasiness.

When they had searched the drawing-room, for instance, he'd not moved a muscle, standing rigid and full of dignity, with his back to the brown marble chimney-piece.

Now, he was watching Maigret as if wondering what the latter could be searching for in his files, but it seemed to be more out of curiosity than fear.

'You certainly have very few patients, Monsieur Serre.'

He made no reply and shrugged his shoulders.

'I notice that there are far more women patients than men.'

The other's expression seemed to say, 'So what?'

'I also see that you first met Maria Van Aerts in your professional capacity.'

He found entries for five visits, spaced over two months, with details of the treatment given.

'Were you aware that she was wealthy?'

A further shrug.

'Do you know Doctor Dubuc?'

He nodded.

'He was your wife's doctor, unless I'm mistaken. Did you recommend him to her?'

Wonders never cease! He was talking at last!

'Doctor Dubuc was treating Maria Van Aerts before she became my wife.'

'You knew, when you married her, that she had heart trouble?'

'She told me about it.'

'Was it serious?'

'Dubuc will tell you if he considers it his duty.'

'Your first wife had a weak heart, too, hadn't she?'

'You'll find her death certificate in the files.'

Janvier was more ill at ease than anyone. He greeted with relief the arrival of the technical experts, who would start a bit of life in the house. As the car drew up in front of the gate, Maigret went to open the door himself, said to Moers under his breath:

'The whole show. Go over the house with a toothcomb.'

And Moers, who'd understood and spotted the bulky form of Guillaume Serre, muttered:

'You reckon that'll shake him?'

'It might end up by shaking someone.'

A few moments later, one might have thought that auctioneers had taken over the house and were preparing to put it up for public sale. The men from the Technical Branch left no corner untouched, taking down the pictures and the photographs, pushing back the piano and the arm-chairs to look underneath the carpets, piling up cupboard drawers, spreading out documents.

Once they caught sight of the face of Madame Serre, who, having taken one glance through the doorway, had withdrawn with a look of distress. Then Eugénie came in grumbling:

'You'll put everything back where it was, I hope?'

She carried on even more when her kitchen was put

through it and even the cupboards where she stored her brooms.

'If only you'd tell me what it is you're looking for.'

They weren't looking for anything in particular. Perhaps, when it came to the point, even Maigret wasn't looking for anything at all. All the time he was watching the man who followed in their tracks and never lost his poise for a second.

Why had Maria written to her friend that Serre was really nothing more than an overgrown schoolboy?

While his men continued to work, Maigret unhooked the telephone and got Dr Dubuc on the line.

'You won't be going out for a while? Can I come and see you? No, it won't take long. Thanks, I'll tell the maid.'

Dubuc had five patients in his waiting-room and promised the Chief-Inspector to let him in by the back door. It was a stone's throw away, along the wharf. Maigret went there on foot, passed the ironmonger's, where the young assistant of the day before hailed him.

'Aren't you going to photograph the ledger?'

'Presently.'

Dubuc was a man of about fifty, with a ginger beard and glasses.

'You attended Madame Serre, didn't you Doctor?'

'Young Madame Serre. Or rather, the younger of the two.'

'You never attended anyone else in the house?'

'Let me see. Yes! A charwoman who'd cut her hand, two or three years ago.'

'Was Maria Serre really ill?'

'She needed treatment, yes.'

'Heart?'

'An enlarged heart. Moreover, she ate too much, complained of dizziness.'

'Did she often call you in?'

'About once a month. Other times she came to see me.'

'Did you prescribe any medicine for her?'

'A sedative, in tablet form. Nothing toxic.'

'You don't think she could have had a heart attack?'

'Most unlikely. In ten or fifteen years, perhaps …'

'Did she do anything to get her weight down?'

'Every four or five months she'd decide to go on a diet, but her resolution never lasted for more than a few days.'

'You've met her husband?'

'Occasionally.'

'What do you think of him?'

'In what way? Professionally? One of my woman patients went to him for treatment and told me that he was very skilful and very gentle.'

'As a man?'

'I thought he seemed of a retiring disposition. What is all this about?'

'His wife has disappeared.'

'Ah!'

Dubuc didn't give a damn, to tell the truth, and he merely sketched a vague gesture.

'These things happen, don't they? He was wrong to put the police on to find her, because she'll never forgive him.'

Maigret didn't argue the point. On his way back, he made a detour so as to pass the garage, which was no longer under observation. The house opposite had been divided into flats. The concierge was outside on the step, polishing the brass knob of the front door.

'Does your window look out on the street?' he asked her.

'What's that got to do with you?'

'I'm a police officer. I wanted to find out whether you knew the person who keeps his car in the garage opposite, the first one on the right.'

'That's the dentist.'

'You see him now and again?'

'I see him when he comes to fetch his car.'

'Have you seen him this week?'

'Here! That reminds me – what was all that messing about in his garage yesterday night? Was it burglars? I said to my husband …'

'It wasn't burglars.'

'Was it you?'

'Never mind. Have you seen him take his car out this week?'

'I believe I did.'

'You don't remember which day? Or what time?'

'It was one night, pretty late. Hang on. I'd got up out of bed. Don't look at me like that. It'll come back to me.'

She seemed to be doing some mental arithmetic.

'I'd just got up out of bed, because my husband had toothache, and I'd given him an aspirin. If he was here he'd tell you straight away what day it was. I noticed Monsieur Serre's car coming out of the garage, and I remember saying what a coincidence.'

'Because your husband had toothache?'

'Yes. And there was a dentist opposite the house at that very moment. It was after midnight. Mademoiselle Germaine had come in. Right, then it was Tuesday, because she only goes out on Tuesday nights, to play cards round at some friends.'

'The car was coming out? It wasn't going in?'

'It was coming out.'

'Which way did it go?'

'Towards the Seine.'

'You didn't hear it stop a little farther on, for instance at Monsieur Serre's house?'

'I didn't take any more notice of it. I'd bare feet and the floor was cold, because we sleep with the window half-open. What's he done?'

What could Maigret have answered? He thanked her and moved away, crossed the little garden, and rang. Eugénie opened the door, giving him a black, reproachful look.

'The gentlemen are upstairs,' she told him curtly.

They'd finished with the ground floor. From upstairs

noisy footsteps could be heard, the rumble of furniture being dragged across the floorboards.

Maigret went up, found old Madame Serre sitting on a chair in the middle of the landing.

'I no longer know where to go,' she said. 'It's like moving house. What can they be looking for, Monsieur Maigret?'

Guillaume Serre, standing in the centre of a room flooded with sunlight, was lighting a fresh cigar.

'My goodness, why did we let her go!' sighed the old lady. 'If I'd only known ...'

She did not state precisely what she would have done had she foreseen the worries that her daughter-in-law's disappearance would bring down upon her.

Chapter Six

IT was twenty to four when Maigret made up his mind, twenty-five past four when the questioning began. But the fateful, almost dramatic moment was that when the decision was taken.

Maigret's behaviour had come as a surprise to those working with him in the house at the Rue de la Ferme. Ever since the morning, there'd been something unusual about the way in which the Chief-Inspector was directing operations. It wasn't the first search of this sort in which they'd taken part, but the more this one proceeded, the more it took on a different nature from any other. It was difficult to define. Janvier, because he knew his Chief better than the others, was the first to feel the change.

When he set them to work there had been a slight, almost fierce flicker of glee in Maigret's eyes; he had loosed them on the house rather as he might have loosed a pack of hounds on a fresh scent, urging them on, not by his voice but by his whole attitude.

Had it become a personal issue between himself and Guillaume Serre? Or more precisely: would events have taken the same course, would Maigret have made the same decision, at the same moment, had the man from the Rue de la Ferme not been heavier than he, physically and morally?

He had seemed, from the start, impatient to get to grips with him.

At other times, one might have attributed different motives to him, wondered if he didn't take a more or less malicious pleasure in turning the house upside-down.

They had seldom been given the chance of working in a home like this, where everything was peaceful and serene, harmonious in a muted minor key, where even the most outdated objects were in no way ludicrous, and where, after hours of exhaustive searching, they hadn't come across even one questionable detail.

When he had made his pronouncement, at twenty to four, they still hadn't found anything. The search party was feeling a certain amount of discomfort, expecting the Chief to withdraw with apologies.

What was it that decided Maigret? Did he know himself? Janvier went so far as to suspect him of having drunk too many *apéritifs* when, about one o'clock, he'd gone to have a bite on the terrace of the café opposite. On his return, it was true, a smell of Pernod could be detected on his breath.

Eugénie hadn't laid the table for her employers. Several times she'd come up to whisper, now in the ear of Madame Serre, now in that of the dentist. At one moment, they'd caught sight of the mother eating, standing up, in the kitchen, as one might during a household removal, and not long after that, Guillaume having refused to come down, the charwoman took him up a sandwich and a cup of coffee.

They were working in the attic by then. This was the most personal part of the house, more personal than the bedrooms and the linen cupboards.

It was enormous, lit by dormer-windows that shed two large luminous rectangles upon the dingy floorboards. Janvier had opened two leather gun-cases, and a ballistics man had examined the weapons.

'These belong to you?'

'They belonged to my father-in-law. I have never done any shooting.'

An hour earlier, in Guillaume's room, they'd found a revolver, which had been examined, and which Maigret had placed on the pile of objects to be taken away for a subsequent check-up.

There was a bit of everything in that pile, including the dentist's professional records and, from an escritoire in the old lady's room, the death certificates of her husband and her first daughter-in-law.

There was also a suit of clothing on which Janvier had

noticed a slight tear in the sleeve, and which Guillaume Serre claimed not to have worn for ten days.

They stumbled about among old trunks, packing-cases, pieces of broken-down furniture which had been taken up to the attic because they were no more use. In a corner stood a child's high chair of an old-fashioned type, with coloured knobs on either side of the tray, and also a rocking-horse, minus tail and mane.

They didn't stop working at lunch-time. The men took it in turns to knock off for a bite, and Moers was satisfied with a sandwich brought to him by the photographer.

Towards 2 p.m., they phoned through to Maigret, from the office, to tell him that a pretty heavy envelope had just come by air from Holland. He had them open it. Inside were Maria's letters, written in Dutch.

'Get hold of a translator and put him to work.'

'Here?'

'Yes. He's not to leave Headquarters until I come.'

Guillaume Serre's attitude had not altered. He followed them about, didn't miss a single action or gesture on their part, but not even once did he seem agitated.

He had a special way of staring at Maigret, and one could see that, for him, the others didn't count. It was indeed a match between the two. The plain-clothes men were merely lay figures. Even the police force didn't count. This was a more personal combat. And in the dentist's eyes one could see an indefinable expression that might have been one of reproach or of contempt.

In any case, he didn't allow this large-scale operation to intimidate him. He raised no more objections, submitted to this invasion of his home and privacy with lofty resignation, in which not the slightest trace of anxiety was perceptible.

Was he a weakling? A tough customer? The two theories were equally plausible. His torso was that of a wrestler, his behaviour that of a self-assured man, and yet, nevertheless, Maria's description of him as an overgrown schoolboy did not appear incongruous. His skin was pale, sickly-looking. In a drawer, they'd found a mass of doctor's prescriptions, pinned together in separate sheafs, some of them dating from twenty years back; the family's medical history could have been reconstructed with the help of these prescriptions, some of which were yellow with age. There was also, in the upstairs bathroom, a small white-painted cabinet containing phials of patent medicine, boxes of pills both new and old.

In this house nothing was ever thrown away, not even old brooms, which were stacked in a corner of the attic beside down-at-heel cracked leather shoes that would never be any use again.

Each time they left a room to launch an attack upon the next, Janvier gave his Chief a look which meant:

'Another wash-out!'

For Janvier still expected to make some discovery. Did Maigret, on the other hand, rely on their finding nothing? He didn't seem surprised, watched them go ahead, puffing lazily at his pipe, sometimes forgetting, for a whole quarter of an hour, to glance round at the dentist.

They realized his decision by implication, and that made it strike them even more forcibly.

Everybody was coming down from the attic, where Guillaume Serre had closed the dormer windows. His mother had just come out of her room to watch them go. They were standing on the landing, in an uneasy group.

Maigret had turned to Serre and said, as if it were the most natural thing in the world:

'Would you mind putting on a tie and a pair of shoes?'

Throughout the day, so far, the man had been wearing slippers.

Serre had grasped his meaning, had stared at him, undoubtedly surprised, but managing not to let it show. His mother had opened her mouth to speak, either to protest or to demand an explanation, and Guillaume had clasped her arm, led her back into her room.

Janvier had asked under his breath:

'You arresting him?'

Maigret had made no reply. He didn't know. To tell the truth, he'd only just made up his mind, on the spur of the moment, here, on the landing.

'Come, in, Monsieur Serre. Will you take a seat?'

The clock on the mantelpiece said four twenty-five. It was a Saturday. Maigret had only realized that from the bustle in the streets, as they crossed the city in a car.

The Chief-Inspector closed the door. The windows were open, and papers on the desk fluttered under the weights that prevented them from blowing away.

'I asked you to sit down.'

He himself went into the wall cupboard to hang up his hat and coat there and to rinse his hands under the enamel fountain.

For the next ten minutes he didn't say a word to the dentist, being too busy signing the things that were waiting on his desk. He rang for Joseph, gave him the file; then, slowly and deliberately, he filled the half-dozen pipes set out in front of him.

It was seldom that anyone in Serre's position could stand it for long without asking questions, losing his nerve, crossing and uncrossing his legs.

At last there was a knock at the door. It was the photographer who'd worked with them all day and been sent on a mission by Maigret. He handed the Chief-Inspector the still damp print of a document.

'Thank you, Dambois. Stay back there. Don't leave without letting me know.'

He waited until the door closed again, lit one of the pipes:

'Would you bring your chair nearer, Monsieur Serre?'

They were now facing each other, separated by the width of the desk, across which Maigret held out the document in his hand.

He added no comment. The dentist took the print,

brought a pair of spectacles out of his pocket, examined it carefully, and put it down on the table.

'I'm waiting.'

'I've nothing to say.'

The photograph was that of a page from the ironmonger's ledger, the one recording the sale of the second sheet of glass and the second half-pound of putty.

'You realize what that implies?'

'Am I to understand that I'm charged?'

Maigret hesitated.

'No,' he decided. 'Officially, you're summoned as a witness. If you wish, however, I am ready to charge you, more exactly to ask the Director of Prosecutions to indict you, which would entitle you to have legal advice.'

'I've already told you that I don't want a lawyer.'

These were only the preliminary moves. Two heavyweights were sizing each other up, taking each other's measure, feeling their way, in the office which had become a sort of ring, and silence reigned in the Duty Room, where Janvier had just put his colleagues in the picture.

'I reckon we're in for a long session!' he told them.

'Think the Chief'll go the limit?'

'He's got that look on his face.'

They all knew what that meant, and Janvier was the first to ring up his wife and tell her not to be surprised if he didn't come home that night.

'Have you a weak heart, Monsieur Serre?'

'An enlarged heart, like yourself, in all probability.'

'Your father died of heart trouble when you were seventeen, didn't he?'

'Seventeen and a half.'

'Your first wife died of heart trouble. Your second wife also had heart trouble.'

'According to statistics, about thirty per cent of people die of heart failure.'

'Your life's insured, Monsieur Serre?'

'Since I was a child.'

'Of course, I saw the policy earlier on. If I remember rightly, your mother is not insured.'

'That's correct.'

'Your father was?'

'I believe so.'

'And your first wife?'

'I saw you take the documents away.'

'Your second wife, as well?'

'It's quite a usual procedure.'

'What is less usual is to keep a sum of several million francs, in gold and currency, in a safe.'

'D'you think so?'

'Can you tell me why you keep this money at home, where it can bring in no interest?'

'I imagine that thousands of people, nowadays, do the same. You forget the financial bills that have resulted several times in a panic, the excessive rate of taxation and the constant devaluations ...'

'I understand. You admit that your intention was to conceal your capital and defraud the Treasury?'

Serre was silent.

'Did your wife – I mean your second wife, Maria – know that this money was shut up in your safe?'

'She did.'

'You told her about it?'

'Her own money was in there as well a few days ago.'

He took his time before answering, weighed his words, let them fall one by one while keeping his eyes fixed gravely on the Chief-Inspector.

'I didn't find any marriage-contract among your papers. Am I to conclude that you were married under the joint-possession laws?'

'That is correct.'

'Isn't that odd, considering your ages?'

'I have already given you the reason. A contract would have obliged us to draw up a balance-sheet of our respective goods.'

'The joint-possession, however, had no existence in actual fact?'

'We each continued to retain control of our own affairs.'

And didn't all this seem quite natural?

'Was your wife wealthy?'

'She is wealthy.'

'As wealthy as you are, or wealthier?'

'About the same.'

'Does she have the whole of her money in France?'

'Only part of it. From her father, she inherited shares in a cheese factory in Holland.'

'In what form did she keep her other assets?'

'Mainly in gold.'

'Even before she met you?'

'I see what you're getting at. Nevertheless, I will tell you the truth. It was I who advised her to sell out her securities and to buy gold.'

'This gold was kept, with yours, in your safe?'

'It used to be.'

'Until when?'

'Tuesday. At the beginning of the afternoon, when she'd nearly finished packing, she came downstairs and I gave her what belonged to her.'

'Then this sum, when she left, was in one of the two suit-cases or in the trunk?'

'I suppose so.'

'She didn't go out before dinner?'

'I didn't hear her go out.'

'So, to your knowledge, she didn't go out?'

He nodded in confirmation.

'Did she telephone at all?'

'The only telephone in the house is in my study, and she did not make use of it.'

'How am I to know, Monsieur Serre, that the money which I found in the safe is *yours alone*, and not yours *and* your wife's?'

Without emotion, still maintaining an expression of

weariness or disdain, the dentist took from his pocket a green notebook which he handed to the Chief-Inspector. Its pages were covered with tiny figures. Those on the left-hand side were headed with the initial O; those on the right with the initial M.

'What does O stand for?'

'Ours. I mean my mother and myself. We've always shared everything, without making any distinction between what is hers and what is mine.'

'The M, I suppose, stands for Maria?'

'You are right.'

'I see a certain figure that occurs at regular intervals.'

'Her share of the household expenses.'

'Every month she paid you the cost of her bed and board?'

'If you like. Actually, she didn't pay me any money, because it was in the safe, but her account was debited with the amount.'

Maigret leafed through the notebook for a few minutes without speaking, got up and went into the room next door, where, like schoolboys, the plain-clothes men immediately pretended to be busy.

He gave instructions to Janvier in a low voice, hesitated as to whether he should have beer sent up for himself, swallowed, as if automatically, the dregs of a glass which stood on Vacher's desk.

When he returned, Serre, who had not moved from his chair, had just lit one of his long cigars and murmured not without insolence:

'D'you mind?'

Maigret was loth to say yes, shrugged his shoulders.

'You've thought about this second window-pane, Monsieur Serre?'

'I haven't bothered to do so.'

'You're wrong. It'd be much better if you could find some reasonable explanation.'

'I'm not looking for one ...'

98

'D'you continue to maintain that you have only once replaced the pane in your study window?'

'The day after the thunderstorm.'

'Would you like us to have the weather-bureau confirm that there was no thunderstorm at Neuilly on Tuesday night?'

'It's pointless. Unless it would give you any satisfaction. I'm speaking of last week's thunderstorm.'

'The day after, you went to the ironmonger's in the Rue de Longchamp and you bought a sheet of glass and some putty.'

'I have told you that already.'

'You are prepared to swear that you haven't been back to the shop since then?'

And he pushed across the desk the photograph of the ledger entry.

'Why, in your opinion, should they have troubled to enter these purchases of glass and putty twice in their book?'

'I've no idea.'

'Why should the shopkeeper state that you came in on Wednesday, about eight o'clock in the morning?'

'That's his business.'

'When did you last use your car?'

'Last Sunday.'

'Where did you go?'

'We took a drive for two or three hours, my mother and I, as is our custom every Sunday.'

'In which direction?'

'Towards the forest of Fontainebleau.'

'Did your wife go with you?'

'No. She wasn't feeling well.'

'You'd decided to separate?'

'There was no question of a separation. She was tired, run down. She didn't always get on with my mother. By mutual agreement we decided that she should go back to her own country for a few weeks or a few months.'

'She took her money with her, all the same?'

'Yes.'

'Why?'

'Because there was a possibility that she wouldn't come back. We're no longer children. We're able to look at life calmly. It is a sort of experiment that we are making.'

'Tell me, Monsieur Serre, there are two frontiers to cross before you reach Amsterdam, aren't there? The French customs, on the way out, are fairly strict about the currency regulations. Wasn't your wife afraid that her gold would be discovered and impounded?'

'Am I obliged to answer?'

'I think it's in your own interests.'

'Even if I risk proceedings?'

'They'd probably be less serious than a charge of murder.'

'Very well. One of my wife's suit-cases was provided with a false bottom.'

'Specially for this trip?'

'No.'

'She'd already had occasion to use it?'

'Several times.'

'To cross the frontier?'

'The Belgian frontier and, once, the Swiss frontier. You're aware, I'm sure, that until just recently it was easier and less expensive to procure gold in Belgium and especially in Switzerland.'

'You admit your complicity in these transfers of capital?'

'I do.'

Maigret got up, went back into the Duty Room.

'Mind coming here a moment, Janvier?'

Then, to Serre:

'My assistant will take down this part of our interview. Please repeat to him word for word what you've just told me. See that he signs his statement, Janvier.'

He went out, got Vacher to show him the office that had been assigned to the translator. He was a little man with glasses who was typing his translation straight on to the machine and pausing from time to time to consult the dictionary that he'd brought with him.

There were at least forty letters, most of them comprising several sheets.

'Where have you begun?'

'At the beginning. I'm on to the third letter. All three are dated about two and a half years ago. In the first one the lady tells her friend that she's getting married, that her future husband is a distinguished man, of imposing appearance, belonging to the highest French professional class, and that his mother looks like I can't remember which painting in the Louvre. I can tell you the name of the painter.'

He turned over the pages.

'A Clouet. Painting is mentioned all the time in these letters. When she's saying what the weather's like, she cites Monet or Renoir.'

'I'd like you to begin at the end, from now on.'

'As you wish. You realize that if I spend all night at it, I won't have finished by tomorrow morning?'

'That's why I'm asking you to begin at the end. What's the date of the last letter?'

'Last Sunday.'

'Can you read it to me quickly?'

'I can give you some idea of it. Wait a moment.

'Gertrude darling,

'Paris has never been so resplendent as this morning and I very nearly went with G. and his mother to the forest of Fontainebleau, which must be adorned with all the glories of a Corot or a Courbet ...'

'Is there a lot about the glories?'

'Shall I skip?'

'Please.'

The translator ran his eyes down a page and moved his lips silently as if in prayer.

'Here you are:

'I wonder what effect returning once again to our Holland and its pastel shades will have upon me and now that the time comes near, I feel I'm being cowardly.

'*After all that I've written to you about my life here, about G. and my mother-in-law, you must be wondering what has happened to me and why I am no longer happy.*

'*It's perhaps because of the dream I had last night, which has spoilt my day. Do you recall the little picture that hangs in The Hague museum and made us blush? It isn't signed. It's attributed to a painter of the Florentine School whose name I have forgotten, and depicts a faun carrying away over his shoulder a completely naked woman who is resisting. You remember?*

'*The faun, in my dream, had G.'s face, and his expression was so fierce that I awoke trembling and bathed in perspiration.*

'*Not with fear, that was the strangest thing. My memory is confused. There was some fear, certainly, but also another emotion. I'll try to explain it to you on Wednesday, when we'll at last be able to chat as we did so much when you came over on your last trip.*

'*I'm to leave on Tuesday night, it's settled. There's no doubt about it. So there are only two more days to wait. I've heaps of things to do during that time. It'll pass quickly. Nevertheless, it seems to me still far away, almost unreal.*

'*Sometimes I have the feeling, especially after that dream, that something will happen to prevent my departure.*

'*Don't worry. My decision is final. I shall follow your advice. I cannot stand this life here for much longer. But ...*'

'You in here, Chief?'

It was Janvier, with sheets of paper in his hand.

'It's done. He's waiting for you.'

Maigret took the papers, left the translator to his task, crossed the Duty Room deep in thought.

Nobody, at that time, could have foretold how long the questioning would take. Guillaume Serre looked up at the Chief-Inspector, took a pen of his own accord from the desk.

'I suppose I have to sign?'

'Yes, here. Have you read it through?'

'I've read it. Might I trouble you for a glass of water?'

'You wouldn't prefer red wine?'

The dentist looked at him, gave the faintest of smiles, inscrutable, heavy with irony and bitterness.

'That, too?' he said disdainfully.

'That, too, Monsieur Serre. You're so afraid of your mother that you are reduced to drink in hiding.'

'Is that a question? I've got to answer?'

'If you wish to.'

'Allow me to inform you, then, that my mother's father was a drunkard, that her two brothers, who are now dead, were drunkards as well, and that her sister ended her days in a lunatic asylum. My mother has lived in fear of seeing me take to drink in my turn, for she refuses to believe that this tendency is not hereditary. When I was a student, she awaited my return with anxiety, and would even sometimes keep a watch on the cafés in the Boulevard Saint-Michel where I was sitting with my friends. There have never been any spirits in the house, and though there's wine in the cellar, she's kept the habit of carrying the key on her.'

'She allows you a glass of wine and water at every meal, doesn't she?'

'I know that she called to see you and spoke to you.'

'Did she tell you what she said to me?'

'Yes.'

'Are you very fond of your mother, Monsieur Serre?'

'The two of us have almost always lived together.'

'Rather like a married couple?'

He coloured slightly.

'I don't know what you mean.'

'Is your mother jealous?'

'I beg your pardon?'

'I'm asking you whether, as often happens with a widow and an only son, your mother shows signs of jealousy towards the people you know. Have you many friends?'

'Has this any connexion with the alleged disappearance of my wife?'

'I didn't find in the house a single letter from a friend, or even one of those group photographs that one sees in most homes.'

He didn't speak.

'Nor is there any photograph of your first wife.'

Still silence.

'Another thing that struck me, Monsieur Serre. The portrait hanging over the mantelpiece is surely of your maternal grandfather?'

'Yes.'

'The one who drank?'

A sign of assent.

'In a drawer I came across a certain number of pictures of yourself as a child and as a young man, also pictures of women and men who must have been your grandmother, your aunt, and your uncles. Always on your mother's side. Doesn't it seem surprising to you that there isn't a single portrait of your father or of his family?'

'It hadn't struck me.'

'Were they destroyed after your father's death?'

'My mother could answer that question better than I.'

'You don't remember if they were destroyed?'

'I was quite young.'

'You were seventeen. What memory have you of your father, Monsieur Serre?'

'Is this part of your interrogation?'

'Neither my questions nor your answers, as you see, are being recorded. Your father was a solicitor?'

'Yes.'

'Did he take personal charge of his practice?'

'Not often. His chief clerk did most of the work.'

'Did he lead a very social life? Or was he exclusively devoted to the family circle?'

'He went about a great deal.'

'He had mistresses?'

'I couldn't tell you.'

'Did he die in his bed?'

'On the stairs, going up to his room.'

'Were you at home?'

'I'd gone out. When I came back, he'd been dead for nearly two hours.'

'Who attended him?'

'Doctor Dutilleux.'

'Is he still alive?'

'He died at least ten years ago.'

'Were you there when your first wife died?'

He drew his heavy brows together, staring at Maigret fixedly, and his lower lip was thrust out in a kind of disgust.

'Answer me, please.'

'I was in the house.'

'What part of the house?'

'In my study.'

'What time was it?'

'About nine p.m.'

'Did your wife keep to her room?'

'She'd gone up early. She didn't feel very well.'

'Had she felt ill for some time?'

'I don't remember.'

'Was your mother with her?'

'She was upstairs as well.'

'With her?'

'I've no idea.'

'Was it your mother who called you?'

'I think so.'

'When you got to the room, your wife was dead?'

'No.'

'Did she die a long time afterwards?'

'Fifteen or twenty minutes later. The doctor was ringing the door-bell.'

'Which doctor?'

'Dutilleux.'

'He was your family doctor?'

'He attended me when I was a child.'

'A friend of your father's?'

'Of my mother.'

'Did he have children?'

'Two or three.'

'You've lost sight of them?'

'I never knew them personally.'

'Why didn't you inform the police that somebody had tried to break open your safe?'

'I had nothing to inform the police.'

'What did you do with the tools?'

'What tools?'

'The ones the burglar left in the room when he made his get-away.'

'I saw neither tools nor burglar.'

'You didn't make use of your car on Tuesday night or early Wednesday morning?'

'I did not.'

'You were unaware that somebody used it?'

'I've had no reason, since then, to go into the garage.'

'When you garaged your car, last Sunday, were there scratches on the boot and the right mudguard?'

'I didn't notice anything.'

'Did you get out of the car, you and your mother?'

He didn't answer for a moment.

'I asked you a question.'

'I'm trying to remember.'

'It shouldn't be so difficult. You were driving along the road to Fontainebleau. Did you set foot to the ground?'

'Yes. We went for a walk in the country.'

'You mean on a country road?'

'A little path running between the fields on the right-hand side of the road.'

'Could you find this path again?'

'I think so.'

'Was it tarred?'

'I don't believe it was. No. That seems unlikely.'

'Where is your wife, Monsieur Serre?'

And the Chief-Inspector rose, not expecting any answer.

'Because we've got to find her, haven't we?'

Chapter Seven

ABOUT five o'clock, already, Maigret had got up for a moment to open the communicating door between his office and the Duty Room and had winked at Janvier. A little later he'd got up again to go and shut the window, despite the heat, because of the noise from outside.

At ten to six he passed through the Duty Room, his jacket over his arm.

'All yours!' he told Janvier.

The latter and his colleagues had grasped the situation a long while ago. From the moment when, at the Rue de la Ferme, the Chief-Inspector had ordered Serre to come along, Janvier was pretty sure that he wouldn't get away from Headquarters very easily. What surprised him was that the Chief had made his decision so abruptly, without waiting to have all the evidence in his hands.

'She's in the waiting-room,' he said under his breath.

'Who?'

'The mother.'

Maigret stationed Marlieux, a young plain-clothes man, who knew shorthand, behind the door.

'Same questions?' asked Janvier.

'The same. And any others that come into your head.'

The idea was to wear down the dentist. The others could take it in turns, go out for a cup of coffee or a pint, make contact with the outside world again, while he would stay as long as need be in the same office, in the same chair.

Maigret began by calling in on the translator, who'd decided to take off his jacket and tie.

'What's she say?'

'I've translated the last four letters. There's a passage in the last but one that might interest you.

'*I've made up my mind, Gertrude dear. I'm still wondering how it came about. Yet I had no dreams last night, or if I had, I have forgotten them.*'

'Does she say much about her dreams?'

'Yes. They're always coming into it. And she interprets them.'

'Go on.'

'*You've often asked me what has gone wrong and I answered that you were imagining things and that I was happy. The truth is that I was trying to persuade myself of it.*

'*Honestly, I've done all I could, for two and a half years, to try and believe that this house was my home and that G. was my husband.*

'*In my heart, you see, I knew that it wasn't true, that I'd always been a stranger here, more of a stranger than I was in the boarding-house you know, where we two spent so many happy hours.*

'*How did I suddenly come to see things really as they are?*

'*Do you remember, when we were little girls? We used to play at comparing everything we saw – people, streets, animals – with the pictures in our photograph albums. We wanted life to be like them. Then, later on, when we began to visit the museums, it was paintings that we used for comparison.*

'*I did the same here, but I did it on purpose, without believing in it, and this morning I suddenly saw the house as it really is, I saw my mother-in-law, I saw G. with a fresh vision, without illusions.*

'*I hadn't had any for some time – I mean illusions. You've got to understand me. I no longer had any, but I stubbornly refused to admit it.*

'*Now that's over. I made up my mind to leave on the spot. I haven't told anyone yet. The old lady hasn't any inkling. She still behaves the same towards me, meek and smiling, so long as I do everything she wants.*

'*She's the most selfish woman I have ever known.*'

'Those words are underlined,' the translator remarked. 'Shall I go on?'

'*As for G., I wonder whether it won't be a relief for him to see me go. He knows that from the beginning we had nothing in common. I could never get used to the feel of his skin, to his smell. Do you understand now why we've never shared the same room, which surprised you so much at the start?*

'*After two and a half years, it's exactly as though I'd just met him in the street or in the underground, and I have the same feeling of recoil whenever he comes to my room. Luckily it doesn't happen often.*

'*I even think, between ourselves, that he only comes because he believes it gives me pleasure, or because he feels it's his duty.*

'*Perhaps it's his mother who tells him to? It's possible. Don't laugh. I don't know how it is with your own husband, but G. has the crestfallen look of a schoolboy who's just been given a hundred lines. Can you see what I mean?*

'*I've often wondered if he was the same with his first wife. It's probable. He would be the same, I expect, with anyone. These people, you see, I mean the mother and son, live in a world of their own and have no need of anybody else.*

'*It seems astonishing that the old lady once had a husband of her own. They never speak about him at home. Besides themselves, there's nobody in the world except the people whose pictures are on the walls, people who are dead, but whom they talk about as if they were more alive than all the living.*

'*I can't stand it any longer, Gertrude. I'll talk to G. presently. I'll tell him that I feel the need to breathe the air of my own country, and he'll understand. What I'm wondering is, how he'll pluck up the courage to tell his mother ...*'

'Is there much more?' asked Maigret.

'Seven pages.'

'Go on translating. I'll be back.'

At the door he turned round:

'When you're hungry or thirsty, ring down to the Brasserie Dauphine. Get them to send up anything you want.'

'Thank you.'

From the corridor he saw, in the glass-panelled waiting-room, old Madame Serre sitting on one of the green velvet chairs. She was bolt upright, her hands folded in her lap. When she caught sight of Maigret, she made as if to get up, but he passed on without stopping and went down the stairs.

The examination had barely begun, and yet it already came as a surprise to see life still going on outside, in broad sunlight, people walking to and fro, taxis, buses with men reading the evening paper on the platform on their way home.

'Rue Gay-Lussac!' he told the driver. 'I'll tell you where to stop.'

The tall trees in the Luxembourg Gardens swayed in the breeze, and all the chairs were taken; there were a lot of bright dresses; some children were still playing along the paths.

'Is Maître Orin at home?' he asked the concierge.

'He hasn't been out for over a month, poor man.'

Maigret had suddenly remembered him. He was probably the oldest solicitor in Paris. The Chief-Inspector had no idea of his age, but he'd always known him as an old man, a semi-invalid, which didn't stop him from always having a smiling face and talking about women with a wicked twinkle in his eye.

He lived, together with a housekeeper almost as old as himself, in a bachelor flat cluttered up with books and prints, which he collected, and most of the prints dealt with bawdy subjects.

Orin was seated in an arm-chair in front of the open window, his knees covered by a rug, despite the weather.

'Well, m'lad? What a pleasant surprise! I'd begun to think everyone had forgotten me or thought that I'd been laid to rest in Père-Lachaise long ago. What's the trouble this time?'

He didn't try to deceive himself, and Maigret coloured slightly, since it was true that he'd seldom called on the lawyer for other than selfish reasons.

'I wondered just now if, by any chance, you would have known a man called Serre who, if I'm not mistaken, died thirty-two or thirty-three years ago.'

'Alain Serre?'

'He was a solicitor.'

'That'd be Alain.'

'What sort of man was he?'

'I suppose I'm not allowed to ask what it's all about?'

'About his son.'

'I never saw the boy. I knew there was a son, but I never met him. You see, Maigret, Alain and I belonged to a gay set, whose life didn't revolve round the family hearth. We were to be found mostly at the club or behind the scenes at variety shows, and we knew all the chorus girls by their Christian names.'

He added, with a ribald grin:

'If you see what I mean!'

'You didn't know his wife?'

'I must have been introduced to her. Didn't she live somewhere in Neuilly? For several years Alain went out of circulation. He wasn't the only one it happened to. There were even a few who looked down on us, once they got married. I didn't expect to see him again. And then, a long time afterwards ...'

'About how long?'

'I don't know. Some years. Let me see. The club had already moved from the Faubourg Saint-Honoré to the Avenue Hoche. Ten years? Twelve years? Anyway, he came back to us. He behaved oddly at first, as if he thought we bore him a grudge for dropping us.'

'Then?'

'Nothing. He went the pace redoubled. Let's see. He went about for a long time with a little singer with a big mouth they used to call ... We had a nickname for her ... Something smutty ... I can't call it to mind.'

'Did he drink?'

'Not more than anyone else. Two or three bottles of champagne occasionally ...'

'What became of him?'

'What becomes of us all in the end. He died.'

'That's all?'

'If you want to know the sequel, m'lad, you'll have to ask aloft. It's St Peter's business and not mine. What misdeed has his son committed?'

'I don't know yet. His wife has disappeared.'

'A gay dog?'

'No. Quite the reverse.'

'Juliette! Bring us something to drink.'

Maigret had to stay another quarter of an hour with the old man, who insisted on trying to find, among his prints, a sketch of the singer.

'I wouldn't swear that it's a good likeness. A very talented chap did it, one night when the whole gang of us were up in his studio.'

The girl was naked and walking on her hands, and her face could not be seen by reason of the fact that her hair was sweeping the floor.

'Come and see me again, Maigret my boy. If you'd had time to share my humble meal ...'

A bottle of wine was warming in a corner of the room and a pleasant smell of cooking filled the flat.

The police at Rouen hadn't been able to pick up Sad Freddie any more than those at Le Havre. Perhaps the expert safe-breaker was no longer in that town. Was he on his way back to Paris? Had he read Ernestine's message?

Maigret had sent a plain-clothes man on a mission along the river-bank.

'Where shall I start from?'

'As far upstream as you can.'

He'd also telephoned his wife that he wouldn't be back to dinner.

'D'you think I'll see you tonight?'

'Probably not.'

He wasn't hoping for too much. He, too, knew that he'd assumed a big responsibility by rushing matters and taking Guillaume Serre down to Headquarters before he had the slightest proof.

Now it was too late. He could no longer let him go.

He felt drowsy, glum. He sat down on the terrace of the Brasserie Dauphine, but, after reading right through the bill of fare, he ended by ordering a sandwich and a glass of beer, for he wasn't hungry.

He went slowly up the staircase at Headquarters. The lights had just come on, although it was still daylight. As his head reached the first-floor level, he glanced automatically at the waiting-room, and the first thing that caught his eye was a green hat that had begun to get on his nerves.

Ernestine was there, sitting opposite Madame Serre, with her hands in her lap like the old lady, and the same air of patience and resignation. She saw him straight away, and deliberately assumed a fixed stare, giving a slight shake of the head.

He understood that she was asking him not to recognize her. Immediately after, she began talking to the old lady as though the ice had been broken some time before.

He shrugged his shoulders, pushed open the door of the Duty Room. The shorthand writer was at work, a pad of paper on his knee. The weary voice of Janvier could be heard, punctuated by his footsteps as he paced up and down the room next door.

'According to you, Monsieur Serre, your wife fetched a taxi on the corner of the Boulevard Richard-Wallace. How long was she away?'

Before relieving him, he climbed up to Moers' attic, where the latter was busy filing documents.

'Tell me, my boy, apart from the brick dust, there were no traces of anything else in the car?'

'The car had been cleaned out very thoroughly.'

'You're sure?'

'It's only by chance that I found a little powdered brick in a fold of the mat, under the driver's seat.'

'Suppose the car hadn't been cleaned and that the driver had got out on a country road.'

'A tarred road?'

'No. Suppose, I'm saying, that he got out, also the person with him, that they'd both gone for a walk on the path and then climbed back into the car.'

'And that it hadn't been cleaned afterwards?'

'Yes.'

'There'd be marks left. Maybe not many. But I'd have found them.'

'That's all I wanted to know. Don't leave yet.'

'Right you are. By the way, I found two hairs in the room of the woman who's disappeared. She was a natural blonde, but gave herself henna rinses. I can tell you what face-powder she used, too.'

The Chief-Inspector went downstairs again, this time went into his office, throwing off his jacket. He smoked a pipe in there all afternoon. Janvier had smoked cigarettes, and Serre cigars. The air was blue with smoke that drifted in a haze up near the light.

'Aren't you thirsty, Monsieur Serre?'

'The Sergeant gave me a glass of water.'

Janvier went out.

'You wouldn't prefer a glass of beer? Or wine?'

Still the same air of bearing Maigret a personal grudge for these little snares.

'Thank you all the same.'

'A sandwich?'

'D'you expect to keep me here much longer?'

'I don't know. Probably. It'll depend on you.'

He went to the door, called out to the plain-clothes men:

'Could one of you fetch me a road-map of the Fontaine-bleau district?'

He was taking his time. All this was just talk, it was merely scratching the surface.

'When you go for a meal, get them to send up some sandwiches and beer, Janvier.'

'Right you are, Chief.'

The road-map was brought to him.

'Show me the spot where you pulled up on Sunday.'

Serre searched for a moment, took a pencil from the desk, marked a cross where the main road met a country lane.

'If there's a farm with a red roof on the left, it'll be this lane here.'

'How long did you go on walking?'

'About a quarter of an hour.'

'Were you wearing the same shoes as today?'

He pondered, looked at his shoes, nodded.

'You're sure about that?'

'Certain.'

His shoes had rubber heels, on which concentric circles were stamped around the maker's name.

'Don't you think, Monsieur Serre, that it'd be simpler and less tiring for you to spill the beans? When did you kill your wife?'

'I didn't kill her.'

Maigret sighed, went to give fresh instructions next door. Couldn't be helped! It'd probably take hours more. The dentist's complexion was already slightly muddier than in the morning, and dark circles had begun to show beneath his eyes.

'Why did you marry her?'

'My mother advised me to.'

'For what motive?'

'For fear I'd be left to live alone one day. She thinks that I'm still a child and that I need someone to look after me.'

'And to stop you from drinking?'

Silence.

'I don't suppose that your marriage with Maria Van Aerts was a love match?'

'We were both nearing our fifties.'

'When did you start to quarrel?'

'We never quarrelled.'

'What did you do with your evenings, Monsieur Serre?'

'I?'

'You.'

'I mostly read, in my study.'

'And your wife?'

'Writing, in her room. She used to go to bed early.'

'Did your father lose much money?'

'I don't understand.'

'Have you ever heard that your father used to lead what they called in those days a fast life?'

'He went about a great deal.'

'Did he spend large sums?'

'I believe so.'

'Your mother made scenes?'

'We're not the sort of people who make scenes.'

'How much did your first marriage bring you in?'

'We don't speak the same language.'

'You and your first wife were married under the joint-possession law?'

'Correct.'

'And she had money. So you must have inherited.'

'Is that unusual?'

'So long as your second wife's body isn't found, you can't inherit from her.'

'Why shouldn't she be found alive?'

'You believe that, Serre?'

'I didn't kill her.'

'Why did you take your car out on Tuesday night?'

'I didn't take it out.'

'The concierge in the house opposite saw you. It was round about midnight.'

'You forget that there are three garages, three former stables, whose doors are adjacent. It was at night, you say so yourself. She may have got them confused.'

'The ironmonger, he couldn't have mistaken someone else for you, in broad daylight, when you went in to buy putty and another window-pane.'

'My word's as good as his.'

'Providing you didn't kill your wife. What did you do with the trunk and the suit-cases?'

'That's the third time I've been asked that question. You've forgotten to mention the tools this time.'

'Where were you on Tuesday about midnight?'

'In bed.'

'Are you a light sleeper, Monsieur Serre?'

'No. My mother is.'

'Neither of you heard anything?'

'I seem to remember telling you that already.'

'And on Wednesday morning you found the house as usual?'

'I suppose that, since an inquiry has been opened, you've the right to question me. You've decided, haven't you, to put me through an endurance test? Your detective has already asked me all these questions. Now it's starting all over again. I can see that it's going to go on all night. To save time, I'll tell you once and for all that I didn't kill my wife. I also inform you that I will not answer any questions which have already been put to me. Is my mother here?'

'What makes you think that she is?'

'Does it seem peculiar to you?'

'She's sitting in the waiting-room.'

'D'you mean to let her spend the night there?'

'I shall make no attempt to prevent her. She's quite free.'

This time Guillaume Serre looked at him with hatred.

'I wouldn't like to have your job.'

'I wouldn't like to be in your shoes.'

They stared at each other in silence, each determined not to lower his gaze.

'You killed your wife, Serre. As you probably killed the first one.'

The other didn't move a muscle.

'You'll confess to it.'

A contemptuous smile curled the dentist's lips, and he threw himself back in his chair and crossed his legs.

Next door the waiter from the Brasserie Dauphine could be heard putting down plates and glasses on a desk.

'I wouldn't mind something to eat.'

'Perhaps you'd like to take off your coat?'

'No.'

He started to eat a sandwich slowly, while Maigret went

to fill a glass with water from the fountain in the wall cupboard.

It was eight o'clock in the evening.

They could see the windows darkening gradually, the view dissolving into specks of light that seemed as far away as the stars.

Maigret had to send out for tobacco. At eleven o'clock the dentist was smoking his last cigar and the air had got more and more thick. Twice the Chief-Inspector had gone out for a stroll through the building and had seen the two women in the waiting-room. The second time they'd drawn their chairs closer together and were gossiping together as if they'd known each other for years.

'When did you clean your car?'

'It was last cleaned a fortnight ago, in a garage at Neuilly at the same time as they changed the oil.'

'It hasn't been cleaned again since Sunday?'

'No.'

'You see, Monsieur Serre, we've just performed a decisive experiment. One of my men who, like yourself, is wearing rubber heels, drove out to the crossing which you marked on the Fontainebleau road. As you stated that you did on Sunday with your mother, he got out of the car and went for a walk along the country lane. It hasn't a tarred surface. He got back in the car and returned here.

'The experts from our technical branch, who're supposed to know their job, then examined the mats in the car.

'Here is the dust and gravel that they gathered up.'

He pushed a small paper bag across the desk.

Serre made no move to take it.

'We'd have found the same thing on the mat in your car.'

'That proves I killed my wife?'

'It proves that your car has been cleaned since Sunday.'

'Couldn't someone have got into my garage?'

'It's unlikely.'

'Didn't your men get in?'

'What are you insinuating?'

'Nothing, Chief-Inspector. I'm not accusing anyone. I'm merely pointing out to you that this operation was undertaken without witnesses, therefore without legal warranty.'

'Wouldn't you like to speak to your mother?'

'You'd love to know what I'd have to say to her? Nothing, Monsieur Maigret. I've nothing to say to her, and she has nothing to say to me.'

A thought suddenly crossed his mind.

'Has she had anything to eat?'

'I've no idea. I can only repeat that she's a free agent.'

'She won't leave as long as I'm here.'

'She may be in for a long stay.'

Serre lowered his eyes and his manner changed. After a long hesitation, he muttered, as if slightly ashamed:

'I suppose it would be asking too much to have a sandwich sent in to her?'

'That was done a long time ago.'

'Did she eat it?'

'Yes.'

'How is she?'

'She talks all the time.'

'To whom?'

'To a certain person who happens also to be in the waiting-room. A girl who used to be on the streets.'

And again there was a gleam of hate in the dentist's eyes.

'You arranged that deliberately, didn't you?'

'Not at all.'

'My mother has nothing to tell.'

'All the better for you.'

They passed the next quarter of an hour in silence, then Maigret plodded into the next-door room, glummer than ever, motioned to Janvier, who was dozing in a corner.

'Same routine, Chief?'

'Anything you like.'

The stenographer was worn out. The translator still worked on in his cubbyhole.

'Go and fetch Ernestine, the one with the green hat, and bring her to Lucas's office.'

When Lofty came in, she didn't look pleased.

'You oughtn't to have interrupted us. She'll start suspecting something.'

Perhaps because it was late at night, Maigret spoke to her more familiarly than usual, without noticing it.

'What've you been filling her up with?'

'How I didn't know why I'd been made to come here, how my husband's been missing two days and I had no news, how much I hate the police and the tricks they're always trying on.

'"They're just keeping me waiting here to try and shake me!" I told her. "They reckon they can get away with anything."'

'What did she say?'

'She asked me if I'd been here before. I said yes, I'd been put through it for a whole night, a year ago, because my husband had had a scrap in a café and they wanted to make out he'd knifed somebody. To start off with, she looked at me like she was sort of disgusted. Then, bit by bit, she began to ask me questions.'

'What about?'

'Mostly about you. I told her everything bad I could think up. I took good care to add that you always managed to make people talk, however tough you had to get with 'em.'

'What!'

'I know what I'm doing. I told her about the time when you kept somebody stark naked in your office for twenty-four hours, in mid-winter, taking care the window was left wide open.'

'There's been no such thing.'

'It shook her. She's less sure of herself than she was when I got here. She spends all her time listening.

'"Does he beat people?" she asked me.

'"It's been known."'

'Would you like me to go back to her?'

'If you want to.'

'Only I'd like to be taken back to the waiting-room by one of the men, and have him be rough with me.'

'Still no news of Alfred?'

'You haven't had any either?'

Maigret had her taken back in the way that she'd asked for and the plain-clothes man returned grinning wryly.

'What happened?'

'Nothing much. When I passed by the old girl, she put up her arm as if she thought I was going to hit her. I'd hardly got out of the room when Lofty burst out crying.'

Madame Maigret rang up to find out if her husband had eaten anything.

'Shall I wait for you?'

'Certainly not.'

He had a headache. He was disgruntled with himself, with everybody else. Perhaps he was a bit uneasy as well. He wondered what would happen if they suddenly received a telephone call from Maria Van Aerts announcing that she'd changed her plans and had quietly settled down in some town or other.

He drank a pint already gone tepid, told them to send up some more before the *brasserie* closed and went back into his office, where Janvier had opened the window. The clamour of the city had subsided. Now and then a taxi crossed the Pont Saint-Michel.

He sat down, his shoulders drooping. Janvier went out. After a long pause, he said musingly:

'Your mother's got it into her head that I'm torturing you.'

He was surprised to see the other raise his head sharply, and for the first time he saw his face look anxious.

'What have they been telling her?'

'I don't know. It's probably the girl who's in there with her. These people like to make up stories so's to seem more interesting.'

'Could I see her?'

'Who?'

'My mother.'

Maigret pretended to hesitate, to weigh up the pros and cons, finally shook his head.

'No,' he said decisively. 'I think I'll question her myself. And I'm wondering if I shouldn't have Eugénie brought down, too.'

'My mother doesn't know anything.'

'Do you?'

'I don't either.'

'Then there's no reason why I shouldn't question her as I've questioned you.'

'Haven't you any pity, Inspector?'

'For whom?'

'An old woman.'

'Maria would have liked to become an old woman, too.'

He walked up and down the office, his hands behind his back, but what he was waiting for didn't come.

'Your turn, Janvier! I'm going to have a crack at the mother.'

Actually he didn't know yet whether he would do so or not. Janvier said later that he'd never known the Chief so tired and so surly as on that night.

It was one in the morning. Everybody at Headquarters had lost confidence, and chagrined glances were exchanged behind the Chief-Inspector's back.

Chapter Eight

MAIGRET was emerging from the Duty Room on his way to look in on the translator when one of the cleaners, who, half an hour before, had invaded the building, came up to tell him:

'There's a lady asking to speak to you.'

'Where?'

'It's one of the two who were in the waiting-room. Seems she's not feeling well. She came into the office I was sweeping out, white in the face like she'd come over queer, and asked me straight off to fetch you.'

'The old lady?' Maigret asked, frowning.

'No, the girl.'

Most of the doors that gave on to the corridor were open. In an office two doors away, the Chief-Inspector caught sight of Ernestine holding one hand to her breast, and strode quickly forward, scowling, his lips framing a question.

'Shut the door,' she whispered when he was within earshot.

And directly he'd done so:

'Phew! I couldn't stick it any longer and that's the truth, but I'm not sick. I put on an act so's to get away from her for a bit. Not that I'm feeling any too bright, either. You wouldn't have a stiff drink about the place?'

He had to go back to his office to get the bottle of brandy that he always kept in the cupboard. Not having any smaller glasses, he poured the spirit into a tumbler and she swallowed it at a gulp, with a shudder.

'I don't know how you manage to take the son. The mother's got me right down. In the finish, I reckoned I'd go crackers.'

'Did she talk?'

'She's wider than me. That's just what I wanted to tell you. To start off I made sure she'd swallowed all the bull I was stuffing her up with.

'Then, I don't know how it happened, she started to pop in a question here and there, all innocent-like. I've been third-degree'd before now and I reckoned I could hold my own.

'With her, I didn't have an earthly.'

'Did you tell her what you were?'

'Not right out. That woman's very, very clever, Monsieur Maigret. How could she have guessed I'd been on the beat? Tell me, does it still show? Then she says to me:

'"You're no stranger to these kind of people, are you?"

'It was your mob she was referring to.

'In the end, she's asking me what it's like in jail, and I'm telling her.

'If you'd told me, when I sat down there in front of her, that I'd give the game away, I'd have refused to credit it.'

'Did you tell her about Alfred?'

'In a way. Without saying exactly what his racket is. She thinks he's a kite-man. She's not all that interested. For three-quarters of an hour now, at least, she's been asking me about life in jail: what time you get up, what you have to eat, what the wardresses act like ... I thought you'd be interested to know and I made out I'd come over queer; I got up saying I was going to ask for a drink, that it wasn't human leaving women to hang about all night ...

'Mind if I have another drop?'

She really was worn out. The brandy brought the colour back into her cheeks.

'Her son won't talk?'

'Not yet. Has she said anything about him?'

'She harks to every sound, gets jumpy every time a door opens. Something else she asked me. She wanted to know if I'd met anybody who'd got guillotined. Now I feel better, I'll go back to her. I'll be on my guard this time, don't worry.'

She took the opportunity to put on some powder, looked at the bottle without venturing to ask for a third drink.

'What's the time?'

'Three o'clock.'

'I don't know how she sticks it. She doesn't look tired, and she's sitting up as straight as at the start of the evening.'

Maigret let her out, took a breath of air at a window opening on to the courtyard, and swallowed a mouthful of brandy out of the bottle. As he crossed the office where the translator was working, the latter showed him a passage that he'd underlined in one of the letters.

'This dates back a year and a half,' he said.

Maria had written to her friend:

Yesterday I had a good laugh. G. came to my room, not for what you might think, but to talk to me about a scheme I'd proposed the day before to go and spend a couple of days in Nice.

They're terrified of travelling, these people. Only once in their lives have they ever been out of France. Their one trip abroad goes back to the time when the father was still alive and they all went over to London together. Incidentally, it appears that they were all seasick and had to call in the ship's doctor.

But that's nothing to do with the case.

Whenever I say something that doesn't suit them, they don't answer straight away. They just stop talking, and, as the saying goes, one can hear a pin drop.

Then, later on or next day, G. comes up to my room, looking distressed, beats about the bush, finally confesses what's worrying him. Briefly, it would seem that my notion of going to Nice for the Carnival was ludicrous, almost indecent. He made no bones about telling me that his mother had been shocked by it and pleaded with me to give up the idea.

Well, it so happened that the drawer of my bedside-table was open. He glanced into it by accident and I saw him turn pale.

'What's that?' he stammered, pointing at the little automatic with a mother-of-pearl butt that I bought during my trip to Egypt.

Do you remember? I wrote to you about it at the time. People had told me that a woman on her own was never safe in places like that.

I don't know why I'd put it in that drawer. I replied coolly:

'It's a pistol.'

'Is it loaded?'

'I don't remember.'

I picked it up. I looked in the magazine. There were no bullets in it.

'Have you any ammunition?'

'There must be some somewhere.'

Half an hour later, my mother-in-law came up on some excuse, for she never enters my room without giving a reason. She also beat about the bush for a while, then explained to me that it was most unseemly for a woman to carry firearms.

'But it's more like a toy,' I retorted. 'I keep it as a souvenir, because the handle's pretty and my initials are engraved on it. I don't think it could harm anybody much, either.'

She gave in, finally. But not before I'd had to give her the box of ammunition that was in the bottom of the drawer.

The funny part is that, no sooner had she gone, than I found in one of my handbags another ammunition-clip that I'd forgotten about. I didn't tell her ...

Maigret, who was holding the brandy bottle in his hand, poured some out for the translator, then he went to give some to the typist and the plain-clothes man who, to try to keep awake, was doodling on his blotter.

When he went back into his office, which Janvier vacated automatically, the bell had gone for another round.

'I've been thinking, Serre. I'm beginning to believe that you haven't been lying as much as I supposed.'

He'd dropped the 'Monsieur', as if so many hours alone together had brought a sort of familiarity. The dentist merely regarded him mistrustfully.

'Maria wasn't meant to disappear any more than your first wife. Her disappearance wasn't to your advantage. She'd packed her bags, announced her departure for Holland. She really intended to take the night-train.

'I don't know if she was supposed to die in the house or not until she got outside. What d'you say to that?'

Guillaume Serre made no reply, but his expression betrayed much more concern.

'If you like it better, she was meant to die a natural death, by which I mean a death that would *pass as natural*.

'This didn't take place, since, if it had, you'd have had no motive for disposing of her body or her luggage.

'There's another thing that doesn't add up. You'd said good-bye to each other. She'd no reason then to go back into your study. Yet her dead body was lying there at a certain time that night.

'I'm not asking you to answer me, but to follow my reasoning. I've only just found out that your wife owned a pistol.

'I'm ready to believe that you shot her in self-defence. After that you got in a panic. You left the body where it had fallen, while you went to get your car out of the garage. It was then, round about midnight, that the concierge saw you.

'What I'm trying to find out, is what changed both your plans and hers. You were in your study, weren't you?'

'I don't remember.'

'That's what you stated.'

'Possibly.'

'I'm convinced that your mother, however, was not in her room, but with you.'

'She was in her room.'

'So you remember that?'

'Yes.'

'Then you remember, also, that you were in your study? Your wife hadn't gone out to fetch a taxi yet. If she'd brought a cab back that night, we'd have found the driver. In other words, it was before leaving the house that she changed her mind and went to your study. Why?'

'I've no idea.'

'You admit that she came to see you?'

'No.'

'You're being unwise, Serre. There are very few instances, in criminal records, when a dead body hasn't been found sooner or later. We shall find hers. And I'm certain, now, that a post-mortem will reveal that she was killed by one or several bullet wounds. What I'm wondering is whether it was a shot fired by your gun or a shot fired by hers.

'The seriousness of your case will depend on that. If the bullet came from her pistol, the conclusion will be drawn that, for one reason or another, she took it into her head to go and settle some score with you and threaten you.

'Money perhaps, Serre?'

He shrugged his shoulders.

'You leaped at her, disarmed her and squeezed the trigger without meaning to. Another theory could be that she threatened your mother and not you. A woman's more likely to feel hatred for another woman than for a man.

'A final possibility, again, is that your own revolver was not in your room, where you put it soon after, but in the drawer of your desk.

'Maria comes in. She's armed. She threatens you. You pull the drawer open and shoot first.

'In either case, you're in no danger of execution. There can be no question of premeditation, since it's quite normal to keep a pistol in the desk of one's study.

'You can even plead self-defence.

'What remains to be explained is why your wife, on the point of leaving, should suddenly have rushed in to see you with a gun in her hand.'

He threw himself back and slowly filled a pipe, without taking his eyes off the other.

'What d'you say to that?'

'This can go on for ever,' said Serre in a tone of disgust.

'You still refuse to talk?'

'I'm answering your questions obediently.'

'You haven't told me why you shot her.'

'I didn't shoot her.'

'Then your mother did?'

'My mother didn't shoot her either. She was up in her room.'

128

'While you were quarrelling with your wife?'

'There was no quarrel.'

'Pity.'

'I'm so sorry.'

'You see, Serre, I've done my best to discover any reason your wife may have had for settling with you and threatening you.'

'She didn't threaten me.'

'Don't be too positive about it, because you may regret your claims later on. It's you who will plead with me or with the jury to believe that your life or your mother's was in danger.'

Serre smiled sardonically. He was tired, slumped in upon himself, his shoulders slightly hunched about his neck, but he hadn't lost any of his self-possession. His beard showed blue through the skin on his cheeks. The sky, beyond the window-panes, was already not quite so dark and the air in the room was becoming cooler.

It was Maigret who felt the cold first and went over to close the window.

'It wasn't to your advantage to have a corpse on your hands. *I mean a corpse that nobody could be allowed to see.* D'you follow me?'

'No.'

'When your first wife died, it was in such a manner that you were able to call in Doctor Dutilleux to make out the death certificate.

'That's how Maria was supposed to die, from apparently natural causes. She had a weak heart too. What had worked once could work again.

'But something went wrong.

'D'you see, now, what I'm getting at?'

'I didn't kill her.'

'And you didn't dispose of her body, together with her luggage and the burglar's tools?'

'There wasn't any burglar.'

'I'll probably confront you with him in a few hours.'

'You've found him?'

His tone was slightly uneasy, all the same.

'We were able to find his fingerprints in your study. You were careful to wipe over the furniture, but there's always some piece that gets forgotten. He happens to be an old offender, an expert in his way, well-known here, Alfred Jussiaume – "Sad Freddie", they call him. He told his wife what he'd seen. She is now out there in the waiting-room with your mother. As for Jussiaume, he's in Rouen and has no further reason to remain in hiding.

'We already have the concierge who saw you take your car out of the garage. We've also got the ironmonger who sold you a second sheet of glass at eight o'clock on Wednesday morning.

'The technical branch will prove that your car has been cleaned since that date.

'That makes quite a lot of evidence, doesn't it?

'When we have found the body and the luggage, my job will be over.

'Then, perhaps, you'll decide to explain why, instead of a, shall we say, lawful corpse, you found yourself landed with a body that you had to dispose of at once.

'There was some hitch.

'What was it, Serre?'

The man pulled a handkerchief out of his pocket, wiped his lips and forehead, but didn't open his mouth to reply.

'It's half-past three. I'm beginning to get fed up. Are you still determined not to talk?'

'I've nothing to say.'

'Very good,' said Maigret, getting up. 'I don't like having to bully an old woman. But I see that I am forced to question your mother.'

He expected a protest, at any rate some display of feeling. The dentist didn't bat an eyelid, and it seemed to Maigret that he even showed a kind of relief, that his nerves relaxed.

'You take over, Janvier. I'll get busy on the mother.'

It really was his intention; he was unable to put it into

practice immediately, for Vacher had just appeared, in great excitement, a parcel in his hand.

'I've got it, Chief! Took me some time, but I think this is it.'

He undid the parcel wrapped in an old newspaper, revealing broken bits of brick, some reddish dust.

'Where?'

'On the Quai de Billancourt, opposite the Île Seguin. If I'd started downstream instead of starting upstream, I'd have been here hours ago. I've been all over the wharves where they unload. Billancourt was the only place where a barge unloaded bricks lately.'

'When?'

'Last Monday. She sailed away about noon on Tuesday. The bricks are still there, and kids must have been playing around, broken a fair amount of them. There's a red dust covering a good bit of the quay. Shall I take it up to Moers?'

'I'll go myself.'

As he went through the waiting-room, he looked at the two women sitting there in silence. It seemed, from their attitudes, as if there was now a chill between them.

Maigret entered the laboratory, where he felt he'd earned a cup of coffee, which Moers had just made.

'Have you got the sample of brick dust? Like to compare them?'

The colour was the same, the pattern seemed identical. Moers used magnifying slides and an electric projector.

'Does it add up?'

'Very likely. Comes from the same district, anyhow. It'll take me about thirty minutes or an hour to do the analysis.'

It was too late to have the Seine dragged. Nor would the River Patrol be able to send a diver down until sunrise. Then, if they found Maria's body, or only the luggage and the tool-box, the circle would be closed.

'Hello! River Patrol? Maigret here.'

He still seemed to be in a bad temper.

'I'd like you to drag the Seine as soon as possible, Quai

131

de Billancourt, at the place where a cargo of bricks was un-loaded recently.'

'In an hour from now it'll be dawn.'

What stopped him from waiting? No jury would ask for further proof to find Guillaume Serre guilty even if he per-sisted in his denials. Without heeding the typist, who was staring at him, Maigret took a long pull at the bottle, wiped his mouth, went out into the passage, and threw open pur-posefully the door of the waiting-room.

Ernestine thought he'd come for her and sprang quickly to her feet. Madame Serre, however, did not move.

It was the latter to whom Maigret spoke.

'D'you mind coming a moment?'

There was a large choice of empty offices. He pushed open a door at random, closed the window.

'Please take a seat.'

And he began to circle round the room, glancing at the old lady sourly from time to time.

'I don't much like to break bad news,' he growled at last. 'Especially to someone your age. Have you ever been ill, Madame Serre?'

'Except when we were seasick, crossing the Channel, I've never had to call in the doctor.'

'So, naturally, you don't suffer from heart trouble?'

'No.'

'Your son does, however?'

'He's always had an enlarged heart.'

'He killed his wife!' he shot out point-blank, raising his head and staring her in the face.

'Did he tell you so himself?'

He hated to use the old trick of a false confession.

'He still denies it, but that won't help. We've got proof.'

'That he's a murderer?'

'That he shot Maria, in his study.'

She had not moved. Her features had stiffened slightly; one had the impression that she'd stopped breathing, but she showed no other sign of emotion.

'What proof have you?'

'We've found the spot where his wife's body was thrown into the river, together with her luggage and the burglar's tools.'

'Ah!'

That was all she said. She was waiting, her hands stiffly folded on her dark dress.

'Your son refuses to plead self-defence. That's a mistake, because I'm convinced that, when his wife entered the study, she was armed and meant to do him harm.'

'Why?'

'That's what I'm asking you.'

'I've no idea.'

'Where were you?'

'In my room, as I told you.'

'You didn't hear anything?'

'Nothing. Only the door closing. Then the sound of a motor engine, in the street.'

'The taxi?'

'I thought it must be a taxi, since my daughter-in-law had said she was going to fetch one.'

'You're not sure? It might have been a private car?'

'I didn't see it.'

'Then it might easily have been your son's car?'

'He swore to me that he didn't go out.'

'You realize the discrepancy between what you're saying now and the statements that you made to me when you called here of your own accord?'

'No.'

'You stated positively that your daughter-in-law went away in a taxi.'

'I still think that she did.'

'But you're no longer certain about it. Are you so certain now that there was no attempted burglary?'

'I saw no sign of any.'

'What time did you come downstairs on Wednesday morning?'

'About half-past six.'

'Did you go into the study?'

'Not immediately. I got the coffee ready.'

'You didn't go and open the shutters?'

'Yes, I believe so.'

'Before your son came down?'

'Probably.'

'You wouldn't swear to it?'

'Put yourself in my place, Monsieur Maigret. For two days I've hardly known where I am. I've been asked all sorts of questions. I've been sitting in your waiting-room for I don't know how many hours. I'm tired. I'm doing my best to hold out.'

'Why did you come here tonight?'

'Isn't it natural for a mother to follow her son in such circumstances? I've always lived with him. He might be in need of me.'

'Would you follow him to prison?'

'I don't understand. I can't believe that ...'

'Let me put it another way: if I made out a charge against your son, would you be willing to share the responsibility for what he did?'

'But since he hasn't done anything!'

'Are you sure of that?'

'Why should he have killed his wife?'

'You avoid giving me a straight answer. Are you convinced that he didn't kill her?'

'So far as I can tell.'

'Is there any chance that he did so?'

'He had no motive for it.'

'But he did!' he said harshly, staring her in the face.

She sat as if in suspended animation. She breathed:

'Ah!'

Then she opened her bag to take out her handkerchief. Her eyes were dry. She wasn't crying. She merely dabbed at her lips with the handkerchief.

'Might I have a glass of water?'

He had to hunt around for a moment, since he didn't know the office as well as his own.

'As soon as the Director of Prosecutions arrives at the Palais de Justice, your son will be indicted. I can tell you now that he hasn't the slightest chance of getting away with it.'

'You mean that he ...'

'He'll go to the guillotine.'

She didn't faint, but sat rigid on her chair, staring blankly ahead.

'His first wife's body will be exhumed. I dare say you know that traces of certain poisons can be found in a skeleton.'

'Why should he have killed them both? It isn't possible. It isn't true, Chief-Inspector. I don't know why you're telling me this, but I refuse to believe you. Let me speak to him. Allow me to talk to him in private and I'll find out the truth.'

'Were you in your room the whole of Tuesday evening?'

'Yes.'

'You didn't go downstairs at all?'

'No. Why should I have gone down, when that woman was leaving us at last?'

Maigret went over for a while to cool his forehead against the window-pane, then walked into the office next door, grabbed the bottle, and drank from it the equivalent of three or four singles.

When he came back, he had assumed the heavy gait of Guillaume Serre and his obstinate glare.

Chapter Nine

HE was sitting in a chair that wasn't his, both elbows on the table, his biggest pipe in his mouth, his eyes fixed upon the old lady whom he'd likened to a Mother Superior.

'Your son, Madame Serre, didn't kill either his first or his second wife,' he said, spacing out the words.

She frowned in surprise, but didn't look any the happier.

'Nor did he kill his father,' he added.

'What do you ...?'

'Hush! ... If you don't mind, we'll settle this as quickly as possible. We'll not bother about proof for the time being. That'll come in due course.

'We won't argue about your husband's case, either. What I'm almost certain of is that your first daughter-in-law was poisoned. I'll go further. I'm convinced that it wasn't done by arsenic or any of the strong poisons that are usually used.

'By the way, Madame Serre, I might tell you that, in nine cases out of ten, poison is a woman's weapon.

'Your first daughter-in-law, like the second, suffered from heart trouble. So did your husband.

'Certain drugs, which wouldn't seriously affect people in good health, can be fatal to cardiac cases. I wonder if Maria didn't provide us with the key to the problem in one of her letters to her friend. She speaks of a trip to England which you once took with your husband, and emphasizes that you were all so badly seasick that you had to be seen by the ship's doctor.

'What would be prescribed in such a case?'

'I've no idea.'

'That's very unlikely. They usually give you atropine in some form or other. Now, a fairly strong dose of atropine can be fatal to a person with a weak heart.'

136

'You mean that my husband ...'

'We'll go into that another time, even if it's impossible to prove anything. Your husband, during his later days, was leading a disorderly life and throwing his money away. You've always been afraid of poverty, Madame Serre.'

'Not for myself. For my son. Which doesn't mean that I would have ...'

'Later on, your son got married. Another woman came to live in your house, a woman who, overnight, bore your name and had as much right there as you.'

She compressed her lips.

'This woman, who also had a weak heart, was rich, richer than your son, richer than all the Serres put together.'

'You believe that I poisoned her, having first poisoned my husband?'

'Yes.'

She gave a little strained laugh.

'Doubtless I also poisoned my second daughter-in-law?'

'She was going away, discouraged, after having tried in vain to live in a house where she was treated like a stranger. Very likely she was taking her money with her. By a coincidence, she had heart trouble, too.

'You see, I wondered from the start why her body disappeared. If she'd simply been poisoned, you only had to call in a doctor who, given Maria's state of health, would have diagnosed a heart attack. Perhaps the attack itself was intended to come on later, in the taxi, at the station, or on the train.'

'You seem very sure of yourself, Monsieur Maigret.'

'I know that something happened which obliged your son to shoot down his wife. Let's suppose that Maria, just as she was going to fetch a taxi or, more likely, as she was on the point of telephoning for one, felt certain symptoms coming on.

'She knew you both, having lived with you for two and a half years. She was a widely read woman, in all sorts of subjects, and it wouldn't surprise me if she had acquired some medical knowledge.

'Realizing that she'd been poisoned, she went into your husband's study while you were in there with him.'

'Why do you say that I was in there?'

'Because, unfortunately for her, she laid the blame on you. If you'd been in your room, she'd have gone upstairs.

'I don't know if she threatened you with her pistol or if she merely reached for the telephone to call the police ...

'There was only one way out for you: to shoot her down.'

'And, according to you, it was I who ...'

'No. I've already told you that it's more likely to have been your son who fired, or, if you'd rather, finished your work for you.'

The drab light of dawn blended with the electric lamps. The lines in their faces were etched more deeply. The telephone bell rang.

'That you, Chief? I've done the test. It's ten to one the brick dust we found in the car came from Billancourt.'

'You can go home to bed, my boy. Your job's through.'

He got up once again, circled the room.

'Your son, Madame Serre, is determined to shoulder all the blame. I don't see any way of stopping him. If he's been able to keep his mouth shut all this time, he's capable of keeping it shut for good. Unless ...'

'Unless ...?'

'I don't know. I was thinking aloud. Two years ago I'd a man as tough as he is in my office and after fifteen hours we still hadn't got a word out of him.'

He threw open the window abruptly, in a kind of rage.

'It took twenty-seven and a half hours to break his nerve.'

'Did he confess?'

'He spilled everything in one long stream, as if it were a relief to get rid of it.'

'I didn't poison anybody.'

'The answer doesn't lie with you.'

'But with my son?'

'Yes. He's convinced that you only did it for his sake, partly out of fear that he'd be left penniless, partly out of jealousy.'

He had to restrain himself from raising his hand to her, despite her age, for the old woman's thin lips had just twitched in an involuntary smile.

'Which is a lie!' he said flatly.

Then, coming closer to her, his eyes on hers, his breath on the woman's face, he rapped out:

'It's not for his sake that you're afraid of poverty, it's for your own! It's not for his sake that you murdered, and if you came here tonight, it's because you were afraid he might talk.'

She tried to shrink away, threw herself back in her chair, for Maigret's face was thrust into hers, hard, menacing.

'Never mind if he does go to prison, or even if he's executed, so long as you can be sure of staying in the clear. You believe that you've still many years to live, in your house, counting your money ...'

She was frightened. Her mouth opened as if to call for help. Suddenly, with a violent, unexpected jerk, Maigret wrenched from her withered hands the bag that she was clinging to.

She gave a cry, shot forward to retrieve it.

'Sit down.'

He undid the silver clasp. Right at the bottom, beneath the gloves, the note-case, the handkerchief, and the powder-compact, he found a folded paper which contained two white tablets.

A hush like that in a church or a cavern enclosed them. Maigret let his body relax, sat down, pressed a bell-push.

When the door opened, he said slowly, without a glance at the plain-clothes man who'd appeared:

'Tell Janvier to lay off him.'

And, as the detective still stood there, in amazement:

'It's all over. She's confessed.'

'I haven't confessed to anything.'

He waited until the door closed again.

'It comes to the same thing. I could have carried on the experiment to the end, let you have the private talk with your son that you wanted. Don't you think that you've caused enough deaths already for one old woman?'

'You meant that I would have ...'

He was toying with the tablets.

'You'd have given him his medicine, or rather what he would have thought was his medicine, and there'd have been no danger of his ever talking again.'

The corners of the roof-tops had begun to be crested with sunlight. The telephone rang again.

'Chief-Inspector Maigret? River Patrol here. We're at Billancourt. The diver's just gone down for the first time, and he's found a pretty heavy trunk.'

'The rest'll turn up as well!' he said indifferently.

An exhausted and astonished Janvier was framed in the doorway.

'They told me ...'

'Take her down to the cells. The man, too, as an accessory. I'll see the prosecutor directly he comes in.'

He'd no longer any business with either the mother or the son.

'You can go off to bed,' he told the translator.

'It's over?'

'For today.'

The dentist was no longer there when he entered his office, but the ash-tray was full of very black cigar-butts. He sat down in his chair and was about to doze off, when he remembered Lofty.

He found her in the waiting-room, where she'd gone to sleep, shook her by the shoulder and, instinctively, she put her green hat straight.

'That's the lot. Off you go now.'

'Has he confessed?'

'It was her.'

'What! It was the old girl who ...'

'Later!' he murmured.

Then, turning round, since he was assailed by a twinge of remorse:

'And thanks! When Alfred comes back, advise him to ...'

But what was the good? Nothing would cure the Sad Man of his mania for burgling the safes that he had once put in, or wean him from his belief that each would be the last and that this time he was really going to live in the country.

On account of her age, old Madame Serre was not executed and left the Court with the complacent air of one who is at last going to set the women's prison in order.

When her son came out of Fresnes jail, after two years, he made straight for the house in the Rue de la Ferme and, that very evening, took the same stroll round the neighbourhood that he'd been accustomed to take in the days when he had a dog to exercise.

He continued to go and drink red wine in the little café and, before entering, to look uneasily up and down the street.

FOR THE BEST IN PAPERBACKS, LOOK FOR THE 🐧

In every corner of the world, on every subject under the sun, Penguin represents quality and variety – the very best in publishing today.

For complete information about books available from Penguin – including Puffins, Penguin Classics and Arkana – and how to order them, write to us at the appropriate address below. Please note that for copyright reasons the selection of books varies from country to country.

In the United Kingdom: Please write to *Dept E.P., Penguin Books Ltd, Harmondsworth, Middlesex, UB7 0DA*.

If you have any difficulty in obtaining a title, please send your order with the correct money, plus ten per cent for postage and packaging, to *PO Box No 11, West Drayton, Middlesex*

In the United States: Please write to *Dept BA, Penguin, 299 Murray Hill Parkway, East Rutherford, New Jersey 07073*

In Canada: Please write to *Penguin Books Canada Ltd, 2801 John Street, Markham, Ontario L3R 1B4*

In Australia: Please write to the *Marketing Department, Penguin Books Australia Ltd, P.O. Box 257, Ringwood, Victoria 3134*

In New Zealand: Please write to the *Marketing Department, Penguin Books (NZ) Ltd, Private Bag, Takapuna, Auckland 9*

In India: Please write to *Penguin Overseas Ltd, 706 Eros Apartments, 56 Nehru Place, New Delhi, 110019*

In the Netherlands: Please write to *Penguin Books Netherlands B.V., Postbus 3507, 1001 AH, Amsterdam*

In West Germany: Please write to *Penguin Books Ltd, Friedrichstrasse 10–12, D–6000 Frankfurt/Main 1*

In Spain: Please write to *Alhambra Longman S.A., Fernandez de la Hoz 9, E–28010 Madrid*

In Italy: Please write to *Penguin Italia s.r.l., Via Como 4, I-20096 Pioltello (Milano)*

In France: Please write to *Penguin Books Ltd, 39 Rue de Montmorency, F-75003 Paris*

In Japan: Please write to *Longman Penguin Japan Co Ltd, Yamaguchi Building, 2–12–9 Kanda Jimbocho, Chiyoda-Ku, Tokyo 101*

BY THE SAME AUTHOR

Maigret and the Madwoman

Maigret's underlings called her the Madwoman. Yet in fact she was a respectable widow – very old, very small – who was convinced that an intruder was shifting about the things in her flat. And she was sure that someone followed her when she spent her afternoons in the park. The old lady claimed that it was a matter of life and death; she demanded an interview with her hero, Chief Superintendent Maigret. From kindness – and a little curiosity – he agreed. But before he can do so, she is murdered . . .

Maigret Sets a Trap

In the oppressively hot streets of Montmartre a murderer has struck five times. The few facts Maigret has at his disposal add up to nothing, yet he must put an end to the fear and speculation. He sets a trap. By feigning an arrest, the true killer may be lured into attempting his sixth slaughter – which he is. But this time Maigret is ready to strike back . . .

Maigret Goes to School

Everyone in Saint-André despised the old postmistress Léonie Birard. She took great pleasure in being spiteful and malicious, in taunting the children and slandering their parents. So nobody regretted her death. Even Gastin, the schoolteacher, accused by the local police and the villagers of shooting her dead. In a desperate bid to prove his innocence, Gastin puts himself under Maigret's protection and begs him to find the real killer . . .

The Patience of Maigret

They called it Maigret's longest investigation. For twenty years there have been a series of daring raids on Paris jewellers. The Superintendent has his suspicions about the organiser – but no proof. Then there is a murder that begins to provide the missing threads . . .

also published:

Maigret on Home Ground